LIMASSOL

Yishai Sarid

LIMASSOL

*Translated from the Hebrew
by Barbara Harshav*

The International

2012

IMPAC
Dublin
Literary Award

Europa Editions
116 East 16th Street
New York, N.Y. 10003
www.europaeditions.com
info@europaeditions.com

Copyright © by Yishai Sarid and Am Oved Publishers Ltd
First Publication 2010 by Europa Editions
Published by agreement with
the Institute for the Translation of Hebrew Literature

Translation by Barbara Harshav
Original Title: *Limassol*
Translation copyright © 2010 by Europa Editions

Library of Congress Cataloging in Publication Data is available
ISBN 978-1-60945-000-7

Sarid, Yishai
Limassol

Book design by Emanuele Ragnisco
www.mekkanografici.com
Cover illustration © Luca Dentale

Prepress by Plan.ed
www.plan-ed.it

Printed in Canada

LIMASSOL

I sat in the car a few more minutes to look at the old picture of her and listen to the end of "Here Comes the Sun." You rarely hear Harrison on the radio, and there aren't many morning songs as good as that one. It's important for me to know the face of a person before I meet them for the first time, so as not to be surprised. She was very beautiful in the picture, hair pulled back in a bun, a wise forehead, smiling at an Arab at some meeting of progressives.

A morning in late July. There was an urban calm of summer vacation in the street. Cats foraging for food in garbage cans, two friends striding to the sea on the tree-lined boulevard, care-free laughter, surfboards under their arm. I live on the third floor, she said on the phone. The mailboxes were covered with layers of stickers, young tenants who came and went and names in Latin letters of people who were no longer alive. The building was rundown and the plaster was peeling. The high narrow windows in the staircase, as in an abandoned monastery, were opaque with dirt. Daphna opened the door barefoot, her hair in a bun, her eyes sharp. That's what I picked up at first glance.

"I'm on the phone," she said. "Come in." I heard the end of a conversation, a brief laugh, a few matter-of-fact words. "I've got to get off now, somebody's waiting for me." I peeped into the living room: two comfortable sofas from the seventies, a big window opening onto the crest of a ficus tree, a small television, interesting works on the walls I didn't have time to examine. The apartment faced the internal courtyard, and was flooded with light. For some reason, I had expected a dark place.

"Come in here, we'll sit in the kitchen," she called.

On the round table was a stack of paper, a bowl of peaches, a handmade colorful cloth. A radio was playing classical music softly in the background, maybe Chopin, maybe somebody I didn't know.

"Why did you come?" she asked. Her voice was surprisingly young.

"I was told you could help me write, you were recommended," I said. "I want to learn how to write."

"That's important to you? You're willing to invest time in that?" she asked quietly, with a restrained smile, and sat down on the chair with one leg folded under her. Now I saw that she was wearing baggy cloth pants.

"Yes, that's why I came."

"You don't work? What do you live on?" she questioned me, and her face was now strong and her look was focused, almost masculine.

"I worked long enough," I said. "Now I want to write. That's what's most important to me." I stuck to my script. I simply couldn't deviate from it now.

"Some people come to me to do the work for them," she said, and put her hands on the table, next to one another. The fingernails were short and clean. "I don't do that. If you want to publish, you'll have to work hard. I won't write for you."

On the sill of the barred kitchen window were pots of herbs. Years of rain and sea spray had cut cracks in the walls; the ceiling was peeling, too.

She asked where I worked, and crossed her legs.

"For thirteen years, I was the director of an investment company," I said. "They were great years in the market. But I left. Maybe someday I'll go back to it. I've got enough money. Now

I'm in a period of creativity. Ever since I was a little boy, I've dreamed of writing a book." I didn't believe such things were coming out of my mouth. Choose a role, I said to myself, decide who you are.

"You've chosen a strange subject for an investment advisor. How did you decide on it?" she asked.

"Look, I studied history at the university," I answered. "Until I had to drop out to earn a living. By chance I came on this article, about an *etrog* dealer in ancient times, and the story stuck with me. I checked the sources and found it in all kinds of forms both in the Talmud and in Hellenistic writings. My imagination is constantly wandering off in his direction."

Her hands were suntanned and narrow, and adorned with thin gold rings, and her eyes were very deep-set; it was hard for me to look into them without feeling embarrassed. She had a long, thin neck with delicate lines, but that didn't bother me, didn't bother me at all. According to the papers, she was seven years older than me. When she went into the army, I was going into fifth grade.

"That's only an outline," she said. "You're at an early stage."

"I'm not in a hurry," I said.

"Your manuscript won't be going to the printer tomorrow," she said. "Tell me what you expect. I don't want awful disappointments. Neither of us could stand that," she laughed. "More people hang themselves because of lack of talent than because of disappointed love."

"Don't worry," I laughed too. "With brokers, it's more common to jump off roofs. I won't hang myself. I just want to write a good book. I'm not a child, and I've got patience. I'm a long distance swimmer."

"I also swim." She shook herself and smiled again. I had managed to draw her out. "Where do you swim?" she asked, interested.

I told her that as a child, I used to swim in the pool at the

Weizmann Institute, I took fifth place in the Israeli youth com-
petition for the five hundred meter crawl. I wasn't an outstanding swimmer, but I did have stamina. We had practice
three or four times a week and I never missed one. Most people
get bored being alone underwater hour after hour, but I
enjoyed the solitude.

"I swim a few times a week," said Daphna. "Two kilometers
each time, sometimes with fins, sometimes with a float on my
legs."

We exchanged data on distances, pools, styles of swimming.
I now understood where her quiet vigor came from. I've always
liked serious swimmers.

She asked where I was from.

"Rehovoth," I answered. "Father a professor of agronomy,
mother a teacher. The standard story."

"There is no standard story," she said. "From that sentence
alone, you could write a thousand novels. I'm sure you've got
something to tell."

Now I blushed, and she saw that and laughed. Watch out, I
said to myself, she's a lot smarter than you.

"How do you want to start?" she asked. A bird perched,
singing in the kitchen window, on top of one of the plants.

"You tell me."

"Maybe we'll talk a little about your hero," she suggested.

"I wrote everything I know about him," I said. "He's a
Jewish trader who travels, after the destruction of the Temple,
to an island in Greece to bring back *etrogs* to the land of Israel."

"You know him?" she asked.

"I think so," I said. "I grew up with him long before I started
writing. There was a time when I traveled abroad a lot on business, and he came with me. Sometimes I myself was an *etrog*
dealer. I checked every version of the story in the library. I also
investigated the island. I was there last year. If there is paradise,
it's in Naxos. And they still grow *etrogs* there."

"What does he look like. What does he think about, what motivates him? What does he eat for breakfast, your *etrog* dealer?" Daphna shot a volley of questions. She kept her youth— in the small space between her teeth, her supple movements, her quick speech.

How did I wind up in this game, I thought. I should have told another story from the start. But there was no other story.

"He's a survivor," I said. "He doesn't think too much. An awful catastrophe happened, and he's just trying to go on with life in his small corner, to bring *etrogs* to *sukkot*. He's a practical man."

"There is no human being who doesn't think too much," she decreed. "You put him on a ship for a two-week trip, and I guarantee you his head is bursting with thoughts. We think a lot more than we act."

I didn't agree with her on that. There are people who keep busy all the time so they won't have to think.

She got up to make coffee. In her kitchen there was nothing new: the stove was old fashioned, the oven was like the one in my grandmother's house in Rehovoth, the refrigerator was an old brand from the sixties. But everything was clean and the light was soft, as if it came from outside through a filter.

"You probably drink coffee with milk," she said. "But I don't have any."

"No," I laughed. "I drink it black."

"You don't look like a banker," she said with her back to me. "Something doesn't fit about you. How many sugars?"

We talked some more about my man, who now sailed from Asia Minor to the island. I described the structure of sailboats at that time, all the details I had checked carefully before I came. She helped me with the ideas.

"Is he married?" she asked. "Does he love somebody?"

"He's thirty-five years old," I answered. "In those days, there were no thirty-five-year-old bachelors. He's got a wife and a lot of children. But he feels good on a trip. The Land of Israel is in an awful condition when he sails off."

"Does he miss his wife very much or does he look at other women on the way?" she laughed.

"Damn! I knew something was missing, got to have sex to sell the book. Maybe I'll put him in bed with a streetwalker in the port of Smyrna before he sails."

"No, no," she laughed and waved her hand in protest. "Don't do that, and definitely don't call her a streetwalker."

I made notes of our conversation on a yellow tablet I thought looked literary. I promised to rewrite the beginning of the story before the next meeting.

I got up and left a hundred shekels on the table, as we had agreed on the phone. She walked me to the door and when I was on my way out, she said quietly: "I don't promise anything. I can't promise the book will be published. You may be paying me for nothing, since nothing may come of this."

"That's perfectly all right as far as I'm concerned. I told you, I'm a big boy."

"I don't want you to be disappointed," she said again. "There are things I can't promise."

"That's all right, Daphna," I called her by name for the first time. We agreed to meet again in a week.

When I got back to the office, I made a short internal email report, and Haim called immediately and told me to come to him. I walked to his office at the end of the corridor, waving to anyone I saw in the offices along the way. As usual, Haim was slumped over, buried behind the computer and the papers.

"How did it go?" he asked. His face was unshaved because of some religious fast.

"Like a private lesson," I said. "She ripped my story to shreds. I don't think I'll make it."

"You've got to," said Haim with a crooked smile. "Your

story really is thin, I told you. I don't know where you got it. *Etrogs* were grown in the Land of Israel, they never had to send anyone to Greece for that."

Once again I showed him the Talmud and he dismissed it. "That's what happens when laymen study Talmud," he said. "They take the soul out of it and leave only the facts. Come study with me once a week and you'll understand the principle." He asked when we'd pull the man out of Gaza.

"Next week," I said. "Maybe another two weeks. After I'm with her the next time. If she agrees to cooperate with us."

"You think she'll agree?" Haim raised his reddened eyes to me.

"I think she has no choice," I said.

"Keep me updated. We're not the only ones in the loop, you know. I want to know every detail."

In her dossier I found old newspaper clippings, good reviews of her first book in the literary supplements, tepid ones for her second book, a picture in the weekend magazine, a girl of twenty-two or -three in a short skirt, eating watermelon next to Dan Ben-Amotz on a veranda in the old city of Jaffa, with big eyeglasses, and beneath it a caption from the gossip page.

There were also undercover pictures taken from a distance with zoom lenses, and they always looked like preparations for clashes: a Jewish-Arab gathering in Nazareth in 1981, a demonstration against the establishment of a settlement in Samaria. She appeared in pictures of four or five such events, but only in one, breathtaking, did the lens focus on her and she appeared in the center of the picture with eyes wide open, illuminated, standing on a narrow road and talking with an old Arab against the background of an olive grove, holding a sign in Hebrew and Arabic. Somebody had been sloppy because no place or date was written anywhere on the picture. In none of the pictures did she look angry, even when people were shouting all around, even when her mouth was open to shout. She was a statistic. Until I started dealing with the issue, she didn't have her own dossier, they had to collect the documents for me from files of other, more important people.

Her first book was about her childhood in Tel Aviv, near the sea, not far from the Carmel Market, a Bulgarian father who was a construction worker and a mother who came alone from Europe after the War. When they gave birth to her the two of them were older and had experienced suffering, but nevertheless, it was a book sparkling with *joie de vivre*. For example, it contained a wonderful chapter about the sea, how her father held her in his arms and went into the water with her the first time. The book came out in 1978, when she was all of twenty-three, and received wonderful reviews that talked about a new and surprising female voice in Hebrew literature, who slaughtered holy cows without sacrificing compassion. I had to look for it in the university library, because there was no trace of it in the bookstores.

The second book was published about two years later, a love story about a young woman and a married man. Apparently it was dreary and too pretentious, it was brought out by a minor publisher and the critics didn't especially like it. I couldn't find a copy of it anywhere, not even in the libraries. After that, she didn't publish anything else, but she edited quite a few books and did translations from English. At a certain period, she taught literature in high school.

For the time being, this was a side job for me and I couldn't give it too much time. Every day, I interrogated detainees, as on an assembly line. I devoted all my attention to them. I talked with them, touched them, breathed stifling air with them—and I didn't look at the clock. Sometimes I stayed at night because there were major arrests and the stench of a terrorist attack was in the air. I tried to talk with Sigi twice a day on the phone. She gave me brief reports about the child. When I expressed interest in what was happening with her, I got only fleeting answers. She knew my mind was somewhere else, that I wasn't really listening. I got home at weird hours, dead tired. Sigi would be sleeping or pretending to be. Early in the morning, while I was still sleeping, if I had even come home, she took the child to kindergarten and went straight to work from there.

I asked them to bring me the last tapes. I had gotten written summaries of all the conversations, but I liked to hear the speech of the target myself, to get close to him, to try to understand the human being. An older woman with a white braid, who looked like a librarian, brought me the tapes. She just sat herself down across from me. I usually worked with Arab prisoners and used monitors in Arabic; I wasn't familiar with her internal branch.

"Interrogators usually don't want to hear the conversations themselves," she said.

"I guess I'm different," I replied.

"I hope you won't give them to anyone," she said with a stern expression.

I raised my head from the papers of the night's interrogation. A guy from Shechem had disappeared from home three days ago, and his father insisted in the interrogation that he didn't know where he was. "Excuse me?" I stared at her.

"Maybe that was unnecessary," she tried to explain. "But working with Jews is different, altogether different. I took the liberty of saying that because this is the first time you've worked with our desk. Leaks are a great risk. You can't know who knows that woman. Maybe somebody lived near her, maybe somebody was in the army with her, we can't know. So we're much stricter about procedures."

"Completely unnecessary," I said. "I didn't start working here yesterday, and I won't be taking the tapes anywhere."

"She sounds like a terrific woman," she muttered. "I once read her book. Not bad. At any rate," and she stood up, "I'm sure you'll be nice to her. Everything is here in the bag. Give it back to us when you're done."

I won't put her on a curved chair with her hands tied behind her, if that's what you mean, I thought. Nor will I put a bag smelling of shit over her head.

Late at night, after a whole day of meetings and evaluations of the attack that took place right under our noses, I dropped the tape in the recorder and listened with earphones. The conversations were continuous and brief. I could jump from one conversation to another, like songs on a CD.

The first conversation was with a certain publisher; they called to ask what was happening with the book she was editing. It's trash for servant girls, she said, and every page was torture for her. Finally she asked about her check, the publisher said there was a problem with an outstanding debt and a garnishment order on the money owed her, she had to take care of that so she could get the money. "What's going on, Daphna?" asked the editor in chief. "How did all those debts get created?" "Drop it," she told him. "You can't help anyway."

Then she talked to a lawyer, who was impatient with her and not very pleasant, and kept saying he was very busy. She pleaded with him, was aggressive, asked when the trial was. The lawyer said they hadn't yet gotten the review of the probation service, that Yotam hadn't made it to a meeting with them. "That's very bad," he stressed. "The probation service is his only hope. You know he's on probation—that judge will toss him in jail without batting an eyelid. I don't think your son is built for jail. They'll eat him alive there. You've got to talk to him, he needs to go to the probation officer, make a good impression, agree to go into a drug rehab program. Otherwise, neither I nor anybody else can help him. Now I've got to go, people are waiting for me."

My ears were burning. I still had to go to the Russian Compound that night to meet some interrogation subjects myself, I didn't see when I'd have a chance to get home. Nevertheless, I played the next conversation.

The man from Gaza spoke good Hebrew. In the conversation with him, Daphna was another woman, completely different: not desperate like the one who talked with the lawyer, not impatient and bitter as in the conversation with the publisher. "How do you feel?" she asked him with concern and warmth. "Still so much pain?"

He told her he went to the seashore that afternoon, somebody drove him. There are families who live on the shore in tents all summer, he said, because it's too stifling in the camps. Whole clans, the women dressed as in Saudi Arabia, go into the water with all their clothes on. He tried to get away from them all a bit, but it was very crowded. Not even the sea helped him anymore.

"Come here, we'll go down to the beach on Gordon Street," laughed Daphna, trying to cheer him up. "You remember how we'd go into the water at night, when you'd teach us the songs of Abd El-Wahab?"

"I want to come," said the man from Gaza. "I miss you, Daphna. Have you got any news about my case?"

"I don't know who to talk to anymore," said Daphna. "I sent letters to everyone I could, I don't know anybody anymore. Once there was somebody in the army that I knew, but he was discharged. I called Shimon Peres's office, they promised to give me an answer. I'm willing to move heaven and earth for you, Hani. I don't know how. It's not like it used to be. Is it my imagination or did it used to be better?"

"It was always shit," he laughed, and he went on in a slow and precise Hebrew. "But at least we could laugh. Today they can shoot you like a dog, let you rot . . . Oh, it hurts, *ya'lan* . . . I'm sorry I curse, Daphna, it hurts too much."

"Don't you have something for the pain?" she asked.

"There's nothing they can give me. The situation is really

bad. Can't sleep at night for the pain. I tried hashish, but it didn't help, just brings bad thoughts, and alcohol is forbidden. I'm waiting for the end now, Daphna. This isn't a life."

"My thoughts are with you," said Daphna quietly. "And I'll get you out of there, don't worry. I'll do whatever it takes. Call me in a few days."

I invested too much time in those literary conversations, suddenly I noticed that it was awfully late. I ran down to the parking lot and dashed onto the freeway toward Jerusalem. My cell phone was full of messages, they called me to come urgently, in the air there was a sense that things were spinning out of control: somebody with a belt of standard explosives and nails was walking around in the area, on lighted streets, in front of cafes, looking for a place with action to set it off, in a crowd of living flesh he would turn into dead flesh, and we couldn't find him.

After I passed Latrun, there was an enormous traffic jam, apparently there had been an accident. I put the blue siren on top of the car and drove up onto the shoulder, the cops at the wreck of the vehicles looked at me and waved me on with their flashlights. I dashed down the slope of Motsa. I opened the window because the heat of the Coastal Plain had dissipated and was replaced by the wind of Jerusalem. The square was empty when I got there, but the spires of the Russian Church were lighted beautifully for the tourists who didn't come. In front of the area of the police station marked off with barbed wire, I got out of the car a moment, called home, asked Sigi to talk with the child. "He fell asleep a long time ago," she said. "Where are you? When are you coming home?"

I went into the human pens to spend the night.

I tried to persuade Haim to take me off that side job. He was one of the last holdouts of his generation in the service—almost fifty years old, one leg crushed in a screwed-up mission in

Lebanon, a workaholic. When I first met him, he didn't wear a *kippa*, even though he always was observant. In recent years he was wearing a black *kippa* again.

"You can put anybody on that file," I said. "Take somebody from the Jewish branch, take somebody from the girls, I don't have time for those literature lessons. I'm running around like a maniac, I haven't taken a shower in two days, I smell worse than the detainees. Do me a favor, Haim, take me off it."

Haim growled that I was the only one who could do that job. Her story is complicated and only I could connect with her background; he couldn't send any of the butchers to her, not even a girl. Besides, I write well. He likes to read the reports of my interrogations, I don't write endless platitudes like the others. And I shouldn't forget that, in my job interview, I told them I was taking a course in creative writing. "It couldn't have sounded worse if you had said you shoot heroin," laughed Haim. "I barely convinced them to accept you. They didn't want such bohemians. They were afraid you were a spy from the press. Aren't you sorry sometimes you didn't become a writer?"

I told Haim to leave me alone.

"You really could have been a writer," he flattered me now. "You've got a discerning eye. The good ones really do use common sense, not force. That takes self-confidence, letting yourself be sensitive, not being swept up in bestiality. Looking at a human being, putting yourself into his head, not putting the bomb in him right away."

I tried to recall the series of detainees from recent days that I had interrogated, and no face was etched in my mind. "I'm losing that, Haim," I said. "I'm also turning into a butcher. I don't have time anymore to be sophisticated with them. You've got to work with force from the first moment. They don't understand you when you're sensitive. They also follow the rules of the game, expect humiliation, beating, pants full of shit, so they'll be justified in talking. They hate us anyway, and they want to earn our hatred honestly. There's too much in the pipeline, there's never a lull. No time for conversations into the night, to give him a cigarette, to hear about his grandfather who escaped on a donkey in the Nakba to arrive slowly to his brother who blew himself up. Elegance is dead, Haim, it's not like it was in your day."

Haim looked at me and seemed a little scared. I didn't usually talk a lot. "You need rest," he said to me distantly. "When was the last time you were home? When did you spend an evening with your wife?"

"Stop it, Haim," I said. "You're talking fantasies. I can't stop the race now, Haim, I don't have to tell you that. Even when I'm home, my mind is down there."

"You've got to rest sometimes," said Haim, with a worried look I had never seen before. "Clean your head, think of other things. At least on the Sabbath. And the holidays are coming. Forbidden to mix prayers with foreign thoughts, forbidden to talk about money. That's why I returned to God. In time, you'll discover the greatness in that. Be with your wife. Sit at the table with her. Have another kid, later you'll be sorry you waited too long. Take a load off your shoulders, nothing will get away from you. And don't beat up anybody. That will destroy you."

Haim's look stayed with me for long hours and many days afterward, but that very evening, as I was getting ready to go home in time to give the child a bath, my cell phone began running hot with more reports about the guy who disappeared, wearing his nice belt, like a bridegroom on his wedding day. I immediately went where I had to go and at dawn I was hoarse from shouting. That night I wasn't sensitive or elegant with anybody.

I got to the second meeting on time, shaved and clean, wearing Bermuda shorts, looking like someone who'd struck it rich in high tech and taken early retirement. I was slightly excited. Going up the stairs, I was gasping. I expected to sit at the table in the cool kitchen, with the smell of rosemary, spin out a conversation about my imaginary text, talk with a cultured and terrific person.

But this time, the apartment was dark, the blinds were closed, she opened the door in a robe as if I had woken her up, her hair was a mess.

"I'm sorry, maybe I got the time mixed up," I muttered awkwardly at the door.

"No, come in," she said with a nod. "Just give me a minute to get myself together. You can sit in the living room. I'll open the window a little."

A bit of light came into the room and she hurried to the inner rooms of the apartment. On the wall was a big print of a Tumarkin, a woman standing in a circle of stones of a sheikh's grave, with a sketch of a cathedral above it. Maybe that's Daphna herself in the picture, twenty years ago. A few minutes later, she came out wearing jeans and a long faded cotton shirt that hid the lines of her body. She was pale and looked exhausted, with dark circles under her eyes. I looked for signs of blows and didn't find any.

"What happened?" I asked.

"Oh, there was a little action," she chuckled. "Uninvited guests came. Sorry about the welcome, I was sleeping a little before you came. Now I'm fine."

"Is there anything I can do to help?" I asked.

Suddenly she looked small and vulnerable, in need of protection. "A few more minutes, OK?" she asked. I heard her walking around the inside rooms and the kitchen, feverishly gathering things and throwing them, opening windows to let in air, destroying evidence of what had happened.

When she came back, her face was more composed and her hair was tied back.

"You're sure . . . "

"Everything's fine," she insisted and furtively changed the props. "Come on, let's talk about your book." She filled the kettle. "I thought about you a little. The subject you've chosen really is interesting, maybe something can be built from it. I hope I didn't discourage you too much. I think we left your man on the ship on the way to the island, right?"

I hadn't had time to write a thing since the previous week, and I'd have to improvise. "I thought of putting in a storm at sea," I said. "But maybe that would be too dramatic."

"Put in drama, I'm for that," she said with an exaggerated laugh. She sat down across from me on the broad sofa. "The Jewish Odysseus, why not . . . " Her mind was definitely not on our meeting. This was the stage in the interrogation where detainees are sent to rest in a cell because it's clear we won't get a single rational sentence out of them.

"I want to tell you something," I said in a quiet voice, as if I were confessing. "I don't know where to go with this story. I feel stuck with it. I almost called you to cancel the meeting today, the whole thing suddenly seemed so artificial. What do I have to do with that? Maybe it's just a fantasy."

An afternoon glow capered in the big back window of the living room, a bird passed by it on its way somewhere, Daphna's look stuck in me and passed beyond me, as if she saw something fateful through me. "You can go," she said.

I searched for a sentence to continue the conversation, struggled with myself not to get up and go to my real work. "You know that feeling?" I asked.

She sat with her arms crossed, folded up in herself. "Of course it's a delusion," she said in a lucid voice. "With real things there is no beauty or reason as in a story. After the first of life's setbacks, you understand that. I wrote a book when I was twenty-three, everything was as clear as a little girl strolling on the shore, easiest thing in the world, like breathing. Now I'm trying to write something new. It's harder than hell. I torture myself. After all, this book won't change the world, I know that, and there's nothing genius about my thoughts, I know that, too. Which leaves the story. But every story has already been told— turn on the television and see all the variations. Nevertheless, I turn out pages and tear them up and am awfully sorry when it doesn't work, sorry enough to cry. Don't know why I'm both- ering you with all this, maybe because I've had two hard days, with people coming and going in my house. You came here for my professional services, and instead I bring you into my life. You listen very well."

I asked: "Who came to your house?" I was mad at myself for not listening to her recent phone conversations.

"People." She looked at me with frozen eyes, but she went on: "They were searching for my son. They were searching for his things in drawers and under the mattress and in the pots in the kitchen. They tore my whole house apart. When they didn't find anything, they took my jewelry. I don't have anything left. They told me that when they found him, they'd cut his throat, that he owed them a lot of money. Here, take the story. Raw material for a novella."

She turned her face toward the big window, the treetop was moving slowly between its corners, and she wept. Maybe I'd reveal myself now, in her moment of weakness, I'd offer the deal.

Too soon, I said to myself. Not professional.

I asked how old he was and what he did in life, even though I knew everything.

"I'm scared they'll catch him," she wept. "Those people have no fear. Say thanks, sweetie, that we don't bash your face in. Maybe we'll break something anyway, as a souvenir, I trem- bled next to them and waited for them to finish me off . . . "

I got up to look for some Kleenex for her. I could never bear women crying; they used tears to buy pity for themselves, or a little more time. It only infuriated me.

"Did you call the police?" I asked.

"I can't call the police. What world do you live in? I can't get my son involved any more than he already is." She went to the bathroom and turned on the faucet again and washed her face and when she came back with her face puffy and red, she said, with a strange laugh: "Don't worry, they aren't your problems. Come on, let's work with your historical tale. Have you thought of who will play your *etrog* merchant in the film?"

"Would you believe," I laughed. "I'm hesitating between Pacino and De Niro. The question is which one would make me more money."

"You're a good fellow," she said with a smile. "I'm glad you came. You're so normal."

She made tea and brought us some dates. Then she put on some quiet new age music in another room, folded her legs under herself on the sofa and asked me about my childhood in Rehovoth, my mother, my father. I told her about the child I was, secret things I had never told, a reward for the lie I wrapped myself in now. Daphna said that if she were me, she would write about those things, take the materials from there, before she'd flee to the *etrogs* of the rabbinic period.

"That doesn't sound so interesting to me," I said. All those memories seemed to be dyed gray and dark blue.

"In the beginning, you don't need a story," she went back to guiding. "Just train yourself on the details. Before you go splashing paint about, making a gigantic picture of Hannibal's battles, you need to know how to draw a horse."

"You think I can ever draw a horse?" I asked.

"Try," she said. "I don't yet know how far you can go."

She gave me a homework assignment for the next meeting. Small exercises for beginners, miniatures of writing on an eggshell. At the door, I asked again if I could help with something, I offered to change the lock. I hadn't yet pulled out the box of solutions.

Daphna smiled, held onto my hand and the bare middle finger with both her thin hands, and said: "It's really good you came. You helped me. See you next week."

I made an urgent request for her recent phone conversations. The woman with the white braid from the Jewish branch brought them to me herself, and again proclaimed how sensitive that material was, that I should take that into account. I almost kicked her out of the office, I didn't know why she suspected me so much, as if I were stamped with some sign I didn't see.

She made call after call, like a madwoman, trying to get hold of some money. Girlfriends rejected her. Sorry, but we don't have anything to give. Some men talked to her very nicely, even offered to meet. I need money, she said firmly, urgently.

"Of course, I understand," one of the voices pounced on the chance. "Come on, let's meet this afternoon and talk about it." She didn't want to meet them this afternoon, or evening, and the conversations ended with nothing.

Afterward, she called her son's friends to find out if they knew where he was, to tell him he had to be careful, that they were looking for him. They all said they hadn't seen him in years, that they hadn't been in touch with him for ages.

In the middle of all that, Hani called from Gaza, asked gently if the people from the Peres center had answered her. On the verge of tears, she replied that she couldn't help him now.

"What happened, Daphna?" he asked her.

"It's the boy," she said. "Problems with him."

"Drugs?" he asked, as if that was a repeat conversation.

There was static on the line in place of her answer.

He coughed a long time and when he calmed down, he said: "I used to play with him. He was such a beautiful child. You said with a laugh that he was ugly, against the evil eye, so nothing would happen to him. I taught him to swim in the sea, remember? He swallowed a little water and got scared, I told him not to be afraid. Too bad I can't see him now. I'd talk with him, he'd understand how lucky he was to be born to you. So he'd know what he's losing . . . "

"I don't know why he hates life so much," sobbed Daphna.

Hani coughed again, at length, tearing up his lungs. I imagined the dirty bed he was lying on, his face sweaty from the disease, the unplastered wall. How did he manage to emit that soft voice?

"I'll call you, Hani," she said in a weepy voice. "When the situation improves a little, we'll talk. Meanwhile, hold on. I'm thinking of you." A sharp beep signaled the end of the conversation.

I wrote Hani's details to our contact in civilian management. A few minutes later, he called back and said there was no problem, they'd take him to Ikhilov Hospital. We're like gods for those people, in one phone call you can save a life. Informers and traitors live longer these days, it's well known; Primo Levi wrote the same thing in his memoirs. "They'll expect him in the oncology department," said the older officer. "He has to come alone to the crossing, just don't let anybody try to play any tricks on us. An ambulance will take him from our side."

I took Haim's suggestion and ordered tickets for Sigi and me for a play on Thursday evening, a time when normal people are starting to calm down after managing to get through another week. My week had no beginning and no end. Sigi dressed up and told me cheerful things about the child, and avoided her usual complaints. When the lights went out, she clung to me and clutched my hand. A few minutes later, my cell phone began quivering against my leg with gentle electric currents. I ignored it. The republic will get along without me for one evening. I tried to immerse myself in the play, but it was old-fashioned and boring and too long. My head wasn't into stories anymore and I couldn't bear a bad ending. Most of the time I looked at Sigi's profile and tried to understand what she was thinking of. Finally, I dozed off a little and woke up with a start now and then when an actor raised his voice too much.

We planned to go eat after the play, the babysitter could stay until twelve. We wanted to talk. Sigi tried with all her might to smile, to be a good friend, not to bother me, to be nice.

"I'll only answer one call and we'll go," I said when we came out to the lobby. I went off to a dark corner, next to the bushes. The conversation went on a long time. I tried to avoid the nightly trip to the interrogation center. I tried to get more and more details on the phone and guide the young fellow who was there. "It won't work," I said at last, angrily. "Hold him downstairs another hour. I'll come to you right away."

When we sat down in the restaurant, I was already starting to glance at my watch. "You aren't coming home tonight?" asked Sigi.

I apologized, explaining the threat in detail. I wanted her to understand. She didn't argue but her face said that wasn't enough for her. She wanted to go.

"I hope I didn't snore too much at the play," I tried to joke. "It really didn't work for me. The characters were too hysterical."

"It's considered a classic," she said quietly, offended, as if she had written it herself.

The restaurant was in downtown Herziliyah Pituah, center of the local nightlife. Groups of people out for the evening passed by in the street, suntanned and calm and dressed up. The waiters explained the daily specials at length. The damn cell phone vibrated again.

I listened to the details of the interrogation and saw Sigi gazing into space. "I'll get back to you soon. Put him in a cell so he'll calm down a little. I'll leave right away," I whispered strongly, to overcome the tumult of the pedestrians in the background.

We hastily ordered our food. I asked about the child, how he was doing in kindergarten. "Fine," she said and picked at her food. I devoured mine because I was very hungry.

"Does everybody there work as hard as you do?" she asked angrily. "Nobody ever goes home?"

"It's a crazy time," I said. "And there are a lot of new people who don't yet know the job. Got to teach them."

"What do you teach them?" Sigi asked quietly. She was sad and down. My feelings for her were like those of a person in freefall, heading down, unable to stop. "How to interrogate, how to get information out of a suspect. Fast. Before the bomb goes off." She was rarely interested in my work, and I wouldn't have told her on my own. I didn't understand where she was leading me now.

"Do they all have bombs?" she asked with a bitter smile I didn't like. "They're all blowing up all the time?"

At the table next to us a jubilant group sat down, men and women about our age, who looked like they could be lawyers. My eyes were caught by one of them, with a spreading baldness and an artificial smile, and he understood that I was looking at him, and muttered something to himself, as if he were cursing me in a whisper, couldn't help looking at Sigi with his small, lustful eyes. I could have sliced him up for that look.

"I thought I might take the child to the sea on Saturday," I said. "I want to teach him to swim."

"Do you beat them up?" asked Sigi.

"Excuse me?"

"Do you beat them up?"

I threw my napkin on the table and said something about protecting her and all the crappy puffed up people sitting around us, so the bomb squad wouldn't have to scrape them off the walls at the end of the evening. A few heads turned to us from the next table, as if I had hit her, at the very least.

"I want to go." Sigi picked up her bag and stood up. I tried to grab her hand, to prevent her, delay her, as if that was the last chance, I even muttered an apology. "Leave me alone," she said. I heard the loathing. I knew it was too late.

We went out into the street separately. She walked ahead quickly. I chased her in damp mists, covered with the sweat of a panicked animal. "You can't walk alone like that at night," I said. "Wait a minute, I'll take you."

"I'm alone all the time," she said. "For years I've been alone." A cab stopped for her and she got in.

"Don't go!" I shouted. "Stop right now." The driver turned his head to me indifferently. I didn't have the power to stop anything here. Sigi quietly told him to go.

I sat in the car in the parking lot, in the dark, and put my head down on the steering wheel. I didn't have the strength to move. I called and she didn't answer. Across from me, under the street lamps, relaxed and satisfied couples passed by, all the weekend pleasures in store for them. I desperately sought faces to talk with. After a lot of calls, she answered. "I'm at home," she said quietly. "The babysitter says the child vomited all evening. Got to go now."

I drove south beneath the orange lights of the freeway. The window was open and the wind whipped hard. I turned on the blue siren on the roof, went through red lights, hurried to get there. Somebody was waiting for me to visit him.

The night guard at the installation knew me, opened the gate, said good evening, asked if I had seen the championship game, they tied with Slovakia, apparently didn't get to the world championship this time either. I bummed a cigarette from him and parked the car inside, next to the iron gate of the interrogation building. I stood outside and smoked. Above me, beams from the spotlights notched the dark. The air smelled salty. Maybe I'd take the child to the sea at Ashkelon, they say the sea is much cleaner there than in Tel Aviv.

I punched in the code and the gate of the installation buzzed open. The British had erected the building in straight, functional lines, with thick concrete walls and big cellars. We made the renovations demanded by technological advances. There was always a smell of shit in the air, despite the disinfectants. I went down the steps until I found the young interrogator who had destroyed my marriage.

"I'm sorry I bothered you on your night off," he greeted me. "But you wanted me to keep you up to date. I couldn't get anywhere with him. He's stubborn as a mule." He had the face of a mechanical engineer, that interrogator, without a trace of sophistication; he didn't have a drop of the poet in him.

"Where is he now?"

"I sent him to the cell, he's sitting there on a stool."

"Ask them to bring him," I said.

The cells were on the bottommost floor, the one the young people call "hell." For twelve years I had been in that business, and hadn't gone down there myself even once. A few soldiers with a low IQ did the hauling for us, and between one thing and another, would lie outside the interrogation rooms like bored Rottweilers, waiting to be called.

In the interrogation room, there was a standard metal desk, a chair for the detainee, a light with a shade full of insect cadavers. Tape recorders were concealed in the wall; there was no window and the air-conditioner was old and rattled. Sometimes you turned it off to hear what the detainee was saying. A single faded poster of wild animals of the Land of Israel was hung on the wall; nobody had the guts to take it down.

The detainee was shoved, blinking, into the room. Downstairs, it was dark. He was a fat fellow with a black beard. They sat him down on the chair with his hands cuffed in back. I offered him water, as I always did at the beginning of the interrogation; they'd always drink. When somebody is thirsty, he doesn't think he'll have to pee in his pants afterward. I asked them to take off his handcuffs. It's better like that, now the two of us are free human beings.

I called him by his nickname, the name of his oldest son. I never went into the interrogation room without reading the file beforehand. I asked how he felt. He drank the water and mumbled something. "What do you say?"

"Hurts a little," he mumbled in Arabic. "I don't feel good."

I said I wanted to send him home, if he'd just tell us where his brother was.

He mumbled into his beard, it was very hard to understand him. There were interrogators who sat with interpreters at their side because they weren't sure enough of their Arabic. I didn't. I learned Arabic in school, afterward I used it in the army for four years, at the university I took courses in the history of the Middle East, and for more than ten years I've been speaking it with the detainees. My Arabic became more and more primitive, the Arabic of the barricades, of simple questions, where and when, why, what did you do there, snarls of monkeys. I didn't have time to read anything worthwhile. I barely understood that fat fellow, he swallowed words.

I took a deep breath, as if nothing was urgent for us, even though his brother was wandering around outside with a corset of nails and steel balls. "How old are you?" I asked, even though I knew the answer.

"Thirty-three." He looked much older, probably from all the baklava and ground lamb.

"And how old is your brother?"

"What brother?" he played innocent, and raised his defiant eyes a little.

"Meroan," I called him by name. "The one who disappeared."

"Oh, he's going on nineteen."

"And where did he go?"

"I really don't know. Maybe to look for work."

The young man was sitting next to me, as if he were at a job interview. His fingers drummed nervously on the table. I was awfully tired, and didn't know how to proceed with the detainee. I tried a direction.

"You love your brother Meroan?" I asked.

"Yes. Love."

"And you don't care that he's going to blow himself up?"

He bowed his head and I saw that his lips were stretched into a smile he couldn't repress.

"You know what happens when a person blows himself up?" I asked. "First of all his head flies into the air like a ball, but the eyes go on seeing for a few more seconds. Can you imagine how scary that is? And then all the internal organs are smeared all around, and the prick flies to hell. Have you ever thought of how such a performance looks?"

He sank into himself. His fingers rolled an imaginary chain of prayer beads and his mouth mumbled chapters of the Koran.

I came close to him. I wanted to attract his attention, so he'd be full of me and what I was telling him. At a certain point, you've got to take up the whole stage.

"That's how concerned you are for your brother?" I whispered to him. "That's how concerned you are for your little brother? What kind of a person are you?"

"Maybe he's scared of what will happen to his brother when they catch him," the young man played the good cop, with a kind of clumsiness that angered me.

"We'll save him," I said into his plump ear. "He'll go to jail for four or five years, get three meals a day, and then he'll go back home. Maybe they'll kidnap some soldier and he'll get out sooner."

My underarms and back were sweating, my shirt was soaked. My detainee was wearing a long black garment, and with the whole beard and the heavy clothing he didn't look as hot as I did. You're a chatterbox, I said to myself, you're entertaining him.

"Did you spend a lot of time together when he was little?" I asked.

He mumbled something again. On his forehead he had those black spots of orthodox worshippers who knock their head on the floor. If you were him, would you inform on your brother who was going to be killed as a martyr? I asked myself.

"What do you love most about him, your brother Meroan?" I asked, and I thought about my child who was vomiting and hadn't fallen asleep tonight. He asks where you are, Sigi said in a café before the play. He needs you. I felt uneasy.

I asked the young man to bring me black coffee. "Can I leave you alone with him?" he answered in a whisper, because it was against procedure.

"No problem," I said. "His legs are bound. He's not going anyplace."

The young man left. I switched off the tape recorder under the table; afterward, I could claim it was a technical screw-up. I moved right on top of the detainee, and stood over him. I had an image of taking out my prick and pissing on him. At that moment, I had no respect for that man, for me he was a fat box concealing a secret that could kill me.

"Listen to me carefully," I said in the most proper Arabic I could come up with. "I will kill you tonight if you don't tell me where your brother is. You won't get to see the light of morning or your wife and children. Listen to me." I grabbed his shirt collar and tightened my grip. "You've got to talk to me, or you'll die. You've got to believe me."

He looked into my eyes furtively and checked me out. His speech was heavy, but his look was intelligent, discerning. I didn't scare him enough, so I had to start hurting him. The slap was harder than I had planned, it stunned him, and then he tried to raise his hands to protect himself, and, still sitting, he got a kick in the stomach. All that was nonsense, as opposed to guts, spilled on pavement. Everything's fine until the wounds are torn open again and organs spill out. The young man came back with the coffee and saw immediately what had happened, understood that I had moved on to the next stage. "No choice, eh?" he whispered to me. "I hope you turned off the tape recorder."

The young man cuffed the detainee's hands to the chair, in a position that arched his back, and I started talking again. "I'll let you go as soon as you say where he is. Do a good Muslim deed. Save your brother, save yourself. Nobody will know you talked. We arrested thirty men to find your brother. Nobody will know it was you."

We left him sitting like that until signs of suffering were seen on his face. In those moments, you want to release them, give them something to drink, maybe they'll be grateful and will talk. But that's a mistake. Now they're only full of awful hatred.

"How many children do you have?" I asked.

"Four," he mumbled. Now sweat was streaming from his forehead. At long last, he felt he was in trouble.

"You want to leave them without a father?" I asked. I had to get into that man's head. Blows won't help crack him, he fled to another world, to places where God was with him, where I couldn't get to at all.

"Why are you mad at us?" I asked, and he smiled again. The young man pushed his shoulder, without permission from me, and got a groan of pain from him. "I'm the only one who touches him," I said.

The young man came close to me and whispered in my ear: "Sorry, but outside, everybody's hysterical. There's information that he's walking around now with the load, that they'll bring him in tonight, but they don't know who. We've got to get it out of him."

Maybe a stick up the ass would do the job now, maybe an electric shock and rats as in South America in the good old days, but I only had my hands and a bag and handcuffs. I didn't have time to dry him out in the cellar. He had to start talking now.

My cell phone started jumping in my pocket and when I looked I saw that Sigi was calling.

"I'll be right back," I said to the young man and went out a moment.

Sigi was crying on the line. Precious time passed until I got her to say that she hadn't slept all night, the child was vomiting and had a fever. "Now he's sleeping?" I asked.

"Now he's sleeping. But that's not why I'm crying," she went on crying, I barely understood what she said.

"Fine, if it's not urgent, let's talk later."

Now I felt pressure in my chest.

"When will you come?" she asked.

"As soon as I finish here." I opened the door of the interrogation room.

"And when will that be?"

"When we catch the man who's planning to blow himself up," I said. I snapped the phone closed and went inside.

I dragged the chair very close to him, breathed his smell, put my face close to him, searched his eyes. "Come on, let's save your brother together," I said. "Help me." And he shook his head hard. He was made of unbreakable material, and even if you chopped him up into pieces, he wouldn't turn into a traitor.

"We're going to bring your wife now," I said. "You know where we'll put her? In a cell with men, rapists and perverts, they're waiting for her there, we bring them a fresh shipment every week. You think I'm joking? You think Jews don't do such things? They do, they do. We've become pigs just like you." I was ashamed of myself, the words coming out of my mouth disgusted me. That detainee was a noble man compared to me. If I'm ever in his situation, I hope I'll have the strength to act just like him.

I signaled to the young man and he tightened the handcuffs even more, and now the detainee was completely twisted back like a bow, his belly remained in front as if it were separate from his body, and a stain of urine spread on his trousers. A real elegant interrogation, I said to myself. I let him dry out like that for a few minutes while I went out to call Sigi, but she didn't answer.

When I came back, the young man was describing, in his halting Arabic, how they'd fuck the prisoner's wife in every hole she had—hard to believe the mouth of that mechanical engineer could utter such words; talk about positions he apparently invented while masturbating in the bathroom. His silence reduced us to nothing more than miserable, pathetic rags.

He started groaning aloud, as if he were about to break. I approached him, I put my hand on his head, I stroked it, coaxing him to talk, to give names and places. It took time for me to understand that he was choking on his own vomit, that his gasps were death rattles.

It took too long for the medic to come; the young man ran to get him, but the medic was outside the gate, eating the food his girlfriend had brought him. We scrambled with the handcuffs that were too tight; the young man ran to get scissors from outside. I tried to straighten him up and get the vomit out of his mouth, but his pupils rolled back, and there was a hanged man's smell of shit coming from him. When the medic arrived, it turned out he didn't have a clue about what to do, an emergency room doctor was needed here. The medic ran to call the doctor on duty, who lived in Ashdod, and by the time he came, we had a fat and stinking corpse lying on the floor and in it the secret we wanted to get out was rotting.

When I left the installation, dawn was already breaking. I filled out the forms you fill out in a situation like that, faxed them where they had to be faxed. I called Haim with my report, he asked me to come to headquarters at eight thirty because the incident had to be investigated, but before that, I should sleep a little, I wasn't going to have an easy day. The young man was in a total panic, saw his career ending before it had even begun.

I told him I'd take full responsibility. As far as I was concerned, he could say he was outside when it happened. Anyway, the only witness was dead and there was no recording. The doctor took us aside, said the man had apparently been particularly sensitive. He didn't think we had deviated from procedures in any way, but the body would be sent for an autopsy and the cause of death would be determined.

The sun was dazzling as soon as it rose over the mountains, and didn't relent for a moment. On the radio, they read announcements from the newspapers, played raucous Hebrew songs. On the side of the road were skeletons of buildings and remnants of yellow fields that could no longer be saved by any rain.

"You've got to rest a little," said Haim in the morning. I was worn out, and my thoughts whisked me away to places I didn't want to be. "I'm not suspending you, I just want you to take some time off from interrogations. Take a break for a few days. There will certainly be small ripples in the coming days, journalists will be interested in it, maybe a member of the Knesset will raise a question. We'll get through that. What's important to me is that you get through it safely, spiritually speaking. It's not simple, I know."

"Spiritually speaking?" I chuckled. "Haim, I offed a human being tonight, I choked him like a pig. And you're talking to me about spirituality? In all that vomit?"

Haim put his hand on mine across the desk. Since the days my father would calm me as a child, no man had touched me like that. My red eyes looked into his weak eyes, and we didn't need to talk anymore. He knew exactly what I was going through now.

"Did you catch him?" I asked.

Haim shook his head. "He's somewhere on the road, apparently they've already put the belt on him. A new gang we don't know are working him, and they maintain good field security. We have no loose end to pull."

"The fact that I couldn't get anything out of him is eating me up," I said. "And I go and finish him off like that."

"If you didn't succeed, nobody could have," he said.

"You're wrong. I'm not fit. There are thoughts that bother me. In a situation like that, you're dragged into violence. That's what happened to me. But I didn't mean to kill him."

"You didn't kill him," said Haim. "Get that out of your head."

They came to recruit me on campus. They investigated me in advance, knew I had been in army intelligence. I knew Arabic, they apparently had good recommendations for me. They knew a few more things, for example, about my opinions back then, because they talked to me about the young peace, how important it was to protect it. I hesitated, I made a weak impression, but Haim insisted and met me two or three times in a café. "You're exactly the kind of people we need," he said. "Not hotheads who only want their beloved country, without the cruelty. I'm not looking for somebody who hates Arabs. As far as I'm concerned, you can love them." He talked with me about Rabin. I asked him for time to think. And then came the attacks of Purim 1996, in the winter, a bus and another one and another one and another one. I heard the number 5 blow up a few streets from the closed-in porch where I was studying for an exam. I saw all the good intentions get lost. I called Haim and told him I agreed, I wanted to protect what was left.

"I want you to focus now on the story of the man from Gaza," said Haim, who looked, behind his desk, like a ball dozing with a *kippa* cover. "Get him out of there fast. We'll start pushing the subject. In a few weeks, things will calm down and then you can go back to normal interrogations, if you want. Rest on the Sabbath as you should, go someplace with your wife. I don't want you to fall apart on me. I really need you."

"You're too forgiving with me," I said.

"Grow up," said Haim. "Take what you deserve. Soften up inside a little and then get strong. Go to your wife now. Come on, get out of here." And he limped with me to the door.

On the way home, a girl from human resources called, said that Haim talked with her, and a room in my name was reserved for the weekend at a hotel at the Dead Sea. I hadn't been at the Dead Sea in years. I called Sigi at work. She said in a tender voice that she'd be glad to go.

Sigi's mother was taking care of the child at home. He felt much better and was glad to see me. The vomiting had stopped. He showed me a new car Sigi had bought him, and tried to make it roll in the air as a friend in kindergarten had taught him. I took a long shower and shaved. My eyes were still red, as if I were weeping, but I knew no tears would come. Afterward, I sat in the kitchen with my mother-in-law, we drank coffee. She asked cautiously if I was very busy. Sigi told her we barely saw each other.

"Maybe now I'll have a little more free time," I said. Her mother was a good woman, a widow, a retired grammar school teacher, and was willing to give her life for her daughter.

"I brought a little food," said the grandmother. "Schnitzel and mashed potatoes, and there's rice in the refrigerator. The doctor said the child should eat rice." I sent her on her way and she hugged and kissed the child, who adored her.

I tried to forget everything and talk with the child about things that had recently happened to him, to give him a piggyback ride, to eat lunch with him. He tried to interest me in his things, took me by the hand, sat me down to look at drawings he had made, I said "very nice, very nice," but I couldn't be clean, I felt as if my brain had been anesthetized. The child felt I wasn't with him, and went off to his own affairs. I sat in the living room and tried to look at the newspaper, which made me so sick—everybody had demands and everybody wanted more money—that I fell asleep. When I woke up, it was almost dark outside and Sigi was standing over me, asking why I had left the child alone.

Friday morning, we went down to the Dead Sea via Jerusalem. The child was belted into his seat in the back.

Sigi asked what had happened that they had released me.

"Haim said I looked too worn out. He doesn't want me to fall apart on him," I told a half-truth.

"Did they find the guy you were looking for?" she asked.

"Not yet."

The vegetation diminished as we went down the mountain, and outside there was a blinding glow. On the sides of the road were places we had once stopped on outings—the strange monastery of Mar Elias, Wadi Kelt, crannies where you could see mountain goats—but now it was dangerous to go there alone with a woman and a child.

Sigi told me about things that had happened to her at work. She worked in the marketing department of a drug company and had just recently gotten a nice promotion. But my mind wandered from her and I didn't really listen.

"So what do you say?" she asked.

"About what?" I stirred.

"About the trip. I think it's a great chance for us."

I apologized and said I hadn't been listening just then.

"They offered to send me to Boston for the company for two years," she said impatiently. "To manage the marketing for the whole east coast. I said I had to talk with you. They're expecting an answer by the end of the month."

"And what about us?"

"What do you mean, what about us? You'd come with me. They're paying for an apartment and all expenses. The salary will also be American. We can live really well on it."

In the oncoming lane a pickup truck with an Arab license plate was speeding. I tensed. The child fell asleep in the back. We were close to the end of the descent, soon we'd turn left to Jericho. The last time I was there was to meet people from Palestinian intelligence; we expected them to inform on their brothers. They slaughtered four lambs for us but they didn't give any real goods. The reserve duty soldier at the army barricade waved us through. I felt sorry for him having to stand outside in that awful heat.

"I've got to think about it," I said. "Right now it doesn't feel real."

"You can finish your doctorate there," said Sigi. "There are loads of universities in the area. I already checked, it could be ideal."

For some reason, an internal rage was burning in me, and the price of controlling it was a heartburn that rose above the windpipe. "I'll think about it," I said again. "Give me a few days."

"You can't imagine how nice it is there, in Boston," she went on.

Mists of heat rose above the valley, and the shoreline of the Dead Sea was farther than I remembered. Instead of a sea, there was a cracked salt marsh and miserable low bushes. "Look how the sea is drying up," I said. "Those maniacs are pumping it for money. The maps aren't right anymore. By the time the child grows up, nothing will be left here."

"It could be better for us there," Sigi persisted. "We need a change of atmosphere. That's also what the doctor told me. Go on a long vacation and get pregnant. He didn't find anything wrong in the examination. You remember how fast I got pregnant the first time."

"So take a leave," I said. "We'll make do on my salary."

"I can't take a leave here," said Sigi. "What would I do on leave? Wait for you to come back at dawn? I can't live day and night with all this tension. The two of us are in this together. It's not just me. You also need to rest. You're the one who insists on another child."

I banged my hand on the steering wheel and a honk blurted out at the curve of the empty road. The child woke with a start. "Sorry," I said quietly. "I want us to enjoy the weekend. Let's leave those things aside."

"You're not well," Sigi hissed behind her sunglasses. "I don't know what you're going through."

But the entrance of the hotel was loaded with groups of fat people lying in armchairs and talking noisily, children running around everywhere—tumultuous like a railroad station where trains don't go anywhere. I gave my name at the reception desk and got the magnetic key card. Sigi carried the child in her arms. We took the elevator up to the room, which was quiet and spacious and had a good view of the sea and the mountains of Moab, or Amnon, one of those nations.

The child woke up when we got to the room, jumped on the big bed until he almost fell, wanted me to pick him up like an airplane, laughed madly. He's a happy child, I said to myself, you mustn't ruin that. Sigi took his car out of the bag. It had been a long time since the three of us were together like that. I wanted to lie down and rest, but the child said he wanted to go to the pool.

"Take him," said Sigi with a weary smile. "I'll stay here and rest." She dressed him in his full bathing suit, which looked like a kind of diving suit, and smeared a thick layer of sunscreen on the exposed parts of his body. I put the water wings on him and put on my own bathing suit and we went downstairs barefoot. The afternoon sun was so strong it burned every thought, and I drowned whatever still threatened to disturb in the clear blue water. We had the pool almost to ourselves because the dining room was already starting to serve lunch and the hotel guests moved there. The child hopped into the water with his skinny legs, spraying to all sides, clung to me, separated from me, wanted me to throw a ball to him, wanted to see me dive to the bottom. I immersed my whole body in the water and observed myself at the same time like a sea lion playing for laughs. It doesn't get any better than this. A blinding thought sliced through me: gather from this moment as much strength as you can.

We went down to examine the sea up close. One man was floating on the water and reading a book, and two women were slowly smearing mud on themselves hoping to preserve their beauty. The child clutched my hand and wanted to see more and more, and I was dragged behind him up and down and into the water and out of it; and in the distance, mists rose up from the land as in the genesis of creation, and the excitement didn't disappear from his face.

We made it back in time to eat lunch leftovers in the dining room. The other guests didn't look so awful now—healthy and happy families, focused on their children. The crowds didn't bother me anymore either. The child devoured a bowl of rice and chicken, and had ice cream for dessert. As I drank my coffee, he came to sit on my lap and his head fell against my chest before I had even finished. I took him to the room and put him gently on the little child's cot, next to our bed.

I hoped Sigi would surprise me in the shower, as she used to, but she was sleeping soundly, and when I came out, I lay down quietly next to her and hugged her. The air-conditioning was silent, the sheets were pleasant, and when the child's jumping around woke me up, it was almost dark outside.

"Good morning," she smiled at me. "We all needed that sleep." I didn't want to open my eyes. The moment was nice. But a dark unpleasant thought passed through me, and even though I was sure it would come true, I tried to ignore it.

Sigi gave the child a shower and washed herself and the three of us went down to the lobby, clean and fragrant. Sigi wanted to drink coffee, and then we looked for the Sabbath service for children conducted by hotel staff.

"What's bothering you?"

"Sabbath peace and blessing," sang the children in the

cellar. Then there was a clown who did magic tricks; he caught me standing in back and tried to drag me onto the small stage, where I would be a victim of his nonsense. No thanks, I gestured, I'm not taking part in this.

"Nothing," I lied to Sigi. "It was great at the pool. The child was very happy."

Sigi held my hand tight and looked at me closely. There was now deafening music in the background. "He loves you very much," said her lips.

At that moment, my beeper went off, and I knew the vacation was over. I read the message and decided to be silent. I had been taken off interrogations, after all. I tried to restrain myself for the sake of the child.

But I wasn't the only one who got the news. Sigi noticed people gathering in the lobby, pressing together around one of the two sofas, whispering, suddenly everyone looked sweaty, and she asked what happened.

"The man we were looking for blew himself up," I said. "In Jerusalem. A few minutes ago. Near a synagogue."

In the lobby began the ceremony of furious expressions, gloomy looks, phone calls to relatives who were liable to be at the site of the disaster. Coarse men and bejeweled women said we should blow them up, and asked how long we had to put up with them. None of that interested me. I would soon have to sit with them for a Sabbath dinner, hear somebody say a blessing, put a napkin on my head, and then eat soup with noodles and fish in sauce. I couldn't stay there anymore. I abandoned the battle out of weakness, I had to hold on and go back.

"I've got to go," I said. "I can't stay here now."

"Where is daddy going?" asked the child.

"To work," Sigi answered wearily. "Maybe you'll take us home," she said quietly. "There's no point to this now anyway."

"Stay, I'll come back here," I said. "Maybe we'll make it back to the pool tomorrow."

I went up to the room to change clothes. I couldn't sit across from a detainee in shorts and sandals. The laments went on around us, but there was also a lively movement toward the dining room.

Sigi asked me to eat dinner with them at least. I sat down impatiently at the table. At the center table, somebody blessed the wine, and everyone stood up. It was crowded and very hot, as if the air-conditioners had stopped working and all the heat of the desert invaded the walls. To get food, you had to stand in a long line. The child sensed my restlessness and he also became nervous, whining that he was hungry, but didn't find anything he liked, and he spilled a glass of juice on himself. "Go," Sigi told me. "Go already. It doesn't do any good for you to be here."

I drove alone to Jerusalem. Outside the area of the hotels, the sky was black and deep, full of stars. A fox ran across the road and I braked to keep from running him over. The soldier at the barricade stood in the middle of the road with a rifle aimed at sixty degrees and waved me to stop. "It's all right, I came through here this morning, with my wife and child," I calmed him.

"Where are they?" he thrust his head into the car, as if I had destroyed them and hidden them in the trunk.

"They stayed at the hotel. I was called urgently to Jerusalem for work," I said.

"Where do you work that you were called on a Friday evening?" asked the nosy reservist, as if we had all the time in the world.

"The secret service," I said.

For some reason, that made him laugh. "Maybe you'll bring me something to eat when you come back, what do you say?"

"No problem, brother, just let me through now."

I went up from the desert on the empty road and got to the city, which was very quiet. Orthodox Jews in Sabbath coats were striding calmly with their sons, ancient pines were waving in the evening wind. The walls of the Old City were lighted up nicely for the tourists who were nowhere to be seen. Silhouettes of the border patrol were walking along dimly lit streets. The serene calm of a silenced city. The explosion was far from here, on the other side of town.

I showed my ID to the guard at the gate of the Russian Compound. An army vehicle unloaded two detainees in handcuffs, their heads covered, who were shoved into the door of the installation. I passed through the corridors and in all of them there was the tumult after the attack, cell phones were coughing, and blindfolded people were shoved and monitors flickered new information. I was glad I had come, I felt comfortable in this tumult.

Haim stood in his Sabbath clothes behind a Formica table and issued orders. When he saw me, he stopped. "What are you doing here? I told you to go rest."

"I came from the Dead Sea," I said. "I can't just sit on my ass."

"You shouldn't have left your wife." Haim gave me a tired look.

"I'm here already," I said.

"They took me away from my spiced fish," grumbled Haim. "There's a lot of pressure in the system. The chief asked me to come direct things myself. So why did you come?"

"I want to interrogate," I said. One of the young men looked at us with curiosity.

"Come here a minute," said Haim, he hopped behind the table and hugged my shoulder. He was a whole head shorter than me. We stood in the corridor in the midst of a convoy of prisoners being shoved inside. "It's not good," said Haim. "I don't want you to interrogate today."

"Haim, don't do this to me," I said. "I know you need me. I've got to correct what I messed up. You leave me alone with my thoughts. Don't retire me at the age of forty. You know there's no going back from this."

"You feel good?" he asked me. We were standing so close I felt his breath blending with mine. His mouth smelled pleasantly of the Sabbath.

"I'll be fine, Haim," I said. "I screwed up. You know I can't be condemned for that."

Haim looked up at me, he had good warm eyes like those of a Turkish singer. "We've brought two of his relatives here," he said. "The two of them were in touch with him in recent days, with that little shit. His film has already made the rounds on the network, with the Kalashnikov and the flag and the parting speech. I know that synagogue. I've got friends who worship there. He put *tsitsis* on his trousers and looked like a good Jerusalem boy. It drives me nuts that he's been walking around under our feet for three days and we didn't catch him. We didn't put a finger on them, his agents. They know the work."

"Who do you want me to take?" I asked.

We were in Jerusalem, so the interrogation rooms had more character. The ceilings were high and the walls were cut from handsome stones. Haim again assigned me one of the young men with a shaved head and greasy skin. Before they brought the prisoner in, we laid out the course of the interrogation, we divided our roles; this time, I tried to go by the book, even though the book never brings results.

The guy they sat in the chair across from me was altogether different from the one I had killed. A trimmed, stylish beard, precise clothes, hair smeared with something shiny. I didn't like him, he looked like a pimp. I figured out immediately that he understood Hebrew from the way his ears were turned to my conversation with the young man. I looked at the papers. In the nineties, when he was young, he spent two months in jail for illegal organizing and hadn't been heard from since.

"We've been looking for you," the young man began in Hebrew.

"Why were you looking?" asked the detainee. "I didn't do anything bad."

Beyond the thick stone walls now came a shout of dread from the other room, and our fellow twisted awkwardly on the chair. For the time being, only his legs were bound.

"Do you know Meroan?" asked the young man.

"Which Meroan?"

"Meroan who blew himself up, who ascended, Meroan with the *tsitsis*," said the young man. His walking back and forth in front of the detainee's face was professional, and managed to make me nervous too.

"I won't tell you no," answered the detainee. For a moment it looked as if it would be easy work with him, maybe I could get back to Sigi tonight.

"Where do you know him from?"

"He's my cousin's son," answered the detainee. "I know him from the village."

"But you haven't lived in the village for years," said the young man. "And he's much younger than you. What do you have to do with him?"

"Nothing special," replied the detainee. His head followed the back and forth movement of the young interrogator, and his eyes rolled nervously. "We'd meet at weddings."

"Great wedding you made for us today," said the young man. Then he waited a moment, as if he were making room for me to get into the interrogation.

I was silent. So far, he was doing fine, why spoil it.

"When was the last time you talked to him?" asked the young man.

"I really don't know, maybe a month ago, two months."

"And if I tell you you talked with him the day before yesterday? You know what is the day before yesterday?" the young man approached the seated detainee, and almost rubbed his belt buckle on his face.

"Of course I know, but that's not so," answered the detainee, as he started playing the game with us.

The young man grabbed his collar until it made a ripping sound, and picked him up a little with one hand. He was a strong fellow. "I'll screw you," he said, "if you don't tell me the truth immediately."

The detainee coughed, fluttered his hands, and said: "Truly, that's the truth," and mumbled something in Arabic.

The young man looked at me again, but I sat and looked on as if I were in a theater. I couldn't get into it. He opened the door and called the soldier waiting behind it, asked him to cuff the detainee's hands in back. Here it comes again, I said to myself.

Meanwhile the young man came to me, his face glowing, and whispered: "I need you now, I feel he's part of the big picture, maybe he knows about the others who are walking around in the area."

The first time was with Haim. He was my guide. I was impressed by his elegance, how he drew close and then moved away, how he applied pressure and let up, hovered before the prisoner like a butterfly, and got everything out of him without ever laying a hand on him. At the climax, there was a sense that he had extracted a cork from a bottle of good and expensive wine.

Elegance has died, I said to myself.

The prisoner was now stretched back like a banana. I felt bad. Wake up, they've been sitting like that here for years, those clients, it's part of the show, that's why they pay for tickets.

The young man scratched his head, looked at me with disappointment, and approached the detainee again. Over and over he asked him about the last conversation, kept shouting he was a liar, but the interrogation didn't get anywhere.

"I should take him downstairs for a few hours, let him cook a little in hell," the young man whispered to me. "But there's no time. That guy is ticking."

"Give me a minute," I stirred and moved into the arena. I pictured the child's happy face in the pool. A heavy price to have to pay for this moment.

"We know you talked with him," I said quietly. He looked at me strangely, almost disparagingly. I had no respect for that pimp; he would rip my heart out without a second thought, if he could.

"A few days ago, a person sat across from me, just like you're sitting now, and I asked him questions. He didn't want to answer. In the middle of our conversation he died. You don't want that to happen to you. So come on, let's talk."

"We talked about the holiday," the detainee blurted out. "He said he was looking to buy a lamb for the family. That's what we talked about."

"I don't think that's what you talked about."

"By my children's lives," said the prisoner. "I'm not involved in those things. I'm careful."

We didn't get anywhere with him and he was starting to control the situation. The young man felt it, too, and stood next to me. If only we could have waited a few hours, we would have broken him with a bag on his head and trance music in the cellar to keep him from sleeping. But there was no time.

"I saw a picture of your wife in your wallet," my partner smiled at him now. "She's a looker, your wife. Let's see," and he shoved a passport photo of a girl with thick lips and long hair in front of his face. "I'd fuck your wife. I can do that tonight. I can ask them to bring her here." We had that now too. We were like a bad theater that puts on a show night after night after night.

A strange expression appeared on the detainee's face. His mouth opened a little, his head was stretched at an angle. It made you want to straighten it, put all the parts back in place.

"So what do you say, Ahmed, me and your wife spending the evening together? She likes to get it hard from behind?" I felt my bile rising, even though I had heard those words countless times. I could see the interrogator next to me changing places with Ahmed, and Ahmed threatening to screw the interrogator's plump wife in the ass. The vision started disintegrating into pixels before my eyes, slivers of a picture, and then I heard the spit and felt it dripping thick on my face, toward my mouth, my fist went out automatically, and the next sound was the crushing of the front teeth of the detainee, Mr. Ahmed. He screamed.

"Why did you do that?" wailed the young man. His image was scattered in pieces before my eyes. "Now we've got to waste time filling out reports, and all those headaches. We were getting ahead with him fine, what came over you?"

"Call the medic," I said. "Then call Haim. Look, I was wounded too." I showed him signs of blood on my knuckles.

I thought of asking his pardon, but that wasn't done. Not far from here they were already gathering up the limbs his little cousin had blown up. He didn't stir any affection either, with his bloody mouth, his whining in pain, the ugly expression on his face. I went on with those thoughts until the medic came in along with Haim, poor Haim. Why did he have to move instead of sitting with his wife and children at the Sabbath table.

We stood outside. The big square of the church was lighted as if they were making a film there. Armored jeeps kept bringing in detainees. "Now it's official," said Haim. "You don't approach detainees anymore. You shouldn't have come here today. I made a mistake when I put you in. Go to your wife now. Be gentle with her. We'll find somebody good you can talk to. I've seen people destroyed in those cellars, I don't want that to happen to you."

I stood before him and was silent. The fist was bleeding a little from the blow. I hit a manacled man. I couldn't even gain any pleasure from the idea that I was fighting for my life. I wanted to go back to the room, release him, give him a fighting chance. Then I could kill him without any pangs of conscience.

Now the streets around the square were silent and the alleys seemed to be presaging something bad. The enormous interchanges out of the city were deserted. I was banished from Jerusalem.

I drove slowly down the turns to the Dead Sea, my hand festering and closed off from the world by a blinding headache. Alone on the road, in the middle of the night, they could easily shoot me, and in my state I wouldn't even get to a gun. An enormous moon shone over the mountains toward the Jordan and lighted the valley. Boston, I thought, I won't ever go to Boston, I won't give up those pleasures. I stopped the car at the side of the road, at the broad opening of the wadi, I got out of the car and yelled my soul to the sky, and the desert birds I startled awake answered me with a shriek.

"I'm done for, *ya habibi*," Hani said to her on the phone. "I can't sleep and can't eat. Save me."

I came to her in the morning. Somebody was sitting in her house. A man with glasses, looked like a literary man, in corduroy pants and sandals.

"This is my livelihood," she said. "Meet him."

Today she was full of self-confidence, wearing gray pants that suited her, a little make-up, arrogant.

"Well then, I'll go," said the man, disappointed. "We'll meet at the party on Thursday. The refreshments will certainly be good. They're always good at rich people's parties. She doesn't stint."

She held out her cheek for a light kiss. "Good luck, Mr. Livelihood," he said as he left. His face was familiar to me from somewhere, but not well-known enough for me to place it.

It won't work, I said to myself. She goes around with a thousand men. The whole plan is fucked. She won't be willing to sacrifice anything for that sick Arab.

"The *etrog* man has arrived," she smiled at me. "Did you

have a good week? Did you earn a lot of money in the stock market?"

"We've got to talk," I said.

An expression of great disappointment rose onto her face. Her look was sharp and hostile.

"Where did you come from?" she asked angrily. "What do you want from me?"

Even though she hated me at that moment, I could have looked into her face forever. Not for nothing do they poison the faces of their women.

"You're not an *etrog* man," she said.

"Not completely," I answered.

"So what do you want from me?" she asked.

"I want to help," I said.

"Another one who wants to help," she laughed briefly. "The one here before you wanted to help, too. I'm surrounded by little helpers today." She quickly regained her equilibrium, didn't let anger take over.

I couldn't cuff her hands behind her, or put the stinking bag on her head. No hands. You're a thug with bad Arabic, a coward, start reinventing yourself. Be a smart Jew.

"Tell me how I can help." I suggested.

Daphna was assailed by a fit of laughter, as if she had smoked something before I came, and when she calmed down, she had tears in her eyes. "Why should I play your game?" Her eyes held me tight. "Maybe you're a maniac, who are you anyway?"

I was silent, and she went on. "You're not a maniac," she said. "You've got the eyes of a poet, not a policeman. I don't care, I'll go on playing with you. Can you fill out any questionnaire I want?"

"Almost any," I said and she laughed again.

"I once had a husband like that," she said. "He was a miracle worker. He's not around anymore, poor guy. What kind of miracle worker are you?"

"What do you want me to do for you?" I insisted.

Somebody in the next building was playing Frank Sinatra. The windows were open. I could have sat in her kitchen forever and looked at her wonderful face.

"You know what I want," she said. "You're gods, you know what a person wants before he says it. You're an angel sent to me."

"Tell me. I can only guess."

"There are two urgent things," she said, and her face became troubled and mature, a hidden line deepened in her forehead now. "I've got a very sick friend," she said. "He lives in Gaza. I want them to take care of him."

"At the Erez Crossing, an ambulance and an entrance permit will be waiting for him on Wednesday. They'll take him from there straight to Ichilov Hospital. You can tell him."

"What do I have to give you in exchange?" she asked in amazement. "Because I'm not willing to pay what I think you want."

"Wait a minute, we haven't yet finished with your wishes. What else do you want?"

"For you to save my son," she growled quickly. "Don't let them kill him, don't let them put him in jail. Resurrect him. You can do that?"

I took a deep breath. That was more than I intended to offer. Talk to her now. "Yes," I said. The reservations were on the tip on my tongue, and I suppressed them. I'm not a crappy lawyer. She nodded slowly and gravely. Her hair was tied on her head.

"You want me to make you something to eat?" she asked calmly, as if we had now signed a successful deal. "I meant to make something anyway. Do you eat tomatoes and Bulgarian cheese?"

She stood erect at the stove, cooked spaghetti in a big pot, deep in thought. I looked at her like a puppy. Then she mixed diced tomatoes with Bulgarian cheese and onion and horseradish, and poured the cold sauce on the cooked spaghetti, and put half a bottle of red wine and a pitcher of cold water on the table. "Eat," she said. "Even people like you deserve to eat."

For six years I had been married to Sigi and never had we eaten so intimately. We drank the wine from little glasses, like people who have lived in an ancient village from time immemorial.

"What do I have to do?" she asked at last. The dishes sat empty before us and so did the bottle of wine.

"Nothing," I said. "Just go on working with me on the *etrog* dealer. A few times a week. I'll call before I come, don't worry. You'll introduce me to your sick friend and say I'm a promising young writer. Or an idiot without any talent who's trying to write, Mr. Livelihood, whatever you choose. I don't care. Just don't hate me."

"Why shouldn't I hate you?" she asked.

"Because my intentions are good."

"I don't believe you." A green spark of suspicion flickered in her eyes. "Do you intend to hurt my friend in some way?"

"No," I answered. "I won't hurt him. I promise you."

"So what do you really want from me?"

"I prefer not to get you involved in that," I said honestly.

"You have to promise me you won't hurt him," she said quietly, her head bent, with the lost pride of someone who has already sold herself.

"I promise."

But she asked me to put that in writing for her. They always want that in writing. Daphna took a sheet of paper from the white pile on the table, and put a pen in my hand. "Write. You promise not to hurt my friend Hani."

I wrote.

And it wasn't a lie, not completely.

Daphna stood up, with the folded note in her hand. I followed every step until she was swallowed up by the entrance to the inner rooms. As long as she didn't call somebody to consult now, that could destroy the whole deal. But she returned a moment later and stood close above my head.

"And I want you to find my son, take care of him. Use force, if you have to. Be a man. Don't cry with him."

"Where is he?" I asked.

"Look in the A-frame huts at the Caesarea shore."

We drank black coffee and she told me about her son. Then she brought me his childhood album, sat down close to me, and took out a few pictures of a teenage boy whose long hair covered his face, his eyes were extinguished. "I don't have any recent pictures," she said. "That's not my fault. He doesn't let himself be photographed."

I walked to the mall under city hall, my head spinning, and a heavy blossoming of bougainvillea in the courtyard stroked my head. I thought of her kitchen, her face that would never grow old. In my pocket I had two pictures of the son. I hurried to pick up my child from kindergarten.

Before I went to him, I went over the dossier again.

A picture in pregnancy and a checked dress, early eighties, from the newspaper *Davar*. The pregnant young writer, at a reception for the aged, well-known Jewish writer Isaac Bashevis Singer on a visit to Israel. Hard to believe how beautiful she was. No man with her. She's holding a glass and a cigarette, laughing.

"Did your beauty help you publish your first book at such an early age, I ask her, and she laughs and bares white teeth," wrote whoever interviewed her for the supplement in *Yediot Aharonot*. You can be the intelligence officer for the woman's paper, I said to myself, and left the room to look for signs of life. There, at the end of the corridor, where they're busy with real things, it's not comfortable for me to show my face now.

Right after the army, she went to New York, worked in an

art gallery, and there she wrote her first book. From a distance, things look clearer, she said to the interviewer in *Yediot*. Two years later, she returned to Israel and started studying literature at the university. Then came the excellent reviews, Dan Meron wrote warmly about her, a strong new female voice in Hebrew literature. After the book was translated into French, she went to Paris for a book tour, and stayed there a few months. Somewhere there was a recording of an interview with her on the French cultural television program, from the early days of video. She had studied French in high school, and her mother had also brought remnants of culture from Europe.

In Paris, I read after lunch, she met Avital Ignats, grandson of the distinguished professor Martin Ignats, one of the founders of Hadassah Hospital and the medical union. At that time, Avital's premiere film was screened at the cinematèques in Paris and Lyon. The film was set in a workers' neighborhood in Haifa. In Israel, the film closed after two weeks, even though it was praised by the critics, who mocked the public that didn't live up to expectations, accusing the audience of provincialism. The film had a foreign flavor, they wrote, lower Haifa looked almost like Naples, Gila Almagor looked like Anna Magnani. They met at an event organized by the Israeli cultural attaché, and moved in together in a garret on a side street on the Left Bank, near the Pantheon. Our reporter in Paris met with them and wrote about two successful young creators who attracted wide attention even abroad.

Somebody passed by my office on the way to the bathroom and poked his nose in. Suddenly I had become the historian of old gossip columns. Vague childhood memories surfaced from reading, men who had disappeared, black and white television programs, Oprah Hazeh the singer from the Ha-Tikvah neighborhood, a new book by David Avidan. My mother, who was fond of culture, followed from our home what was going on in bohemian circles.

A picture of them in April 1980, shortly after they returned to Israel to film Ignats's new movie. The two of them wearing white, in the background the masts of the port of Jaffa. You could smell her fresh scent from the yellowing paper, tanned legs in a mini skirt, clear smile. Soon her second book will be published, Avital directs an Israeli and international cast of actors on a set, wearing sunglasses, like Antonioni . . .

"I see you're deep into that," Haim stood in the door and smiled.

"Look what you've done to me," I laughed. "You could have cut off my hand so I couldn't hit anymore instead."

"There were ideas like that," said Haim. "We got a letter from the association for citizen rights suggesting that, for you, we bring back the guillotine."

Haim sat down across from me, his body filling the little room, and said the matter was starting to get urgent, unpleasant information was coming in from army intelligence. "When will the father from Gaza come?" he asked.

"Day after tomorrow," I said. "Everything's arranged with the hospital. Everything's arranged with the lady."

"Everything went smoothly with her?" asked Haim. "What did she want?"

"She wants me to save her son."

Haim tried to relieve his gimpy leg. "What's with her son?"

"All the big problems," I said. "Drugs mainly. He owes a lot of money to criminals."

"How will you save him?" asked Haim.

"No idea," I said. "I've never seen a junkie who really managed to kick the habit."

"So why did you promise her?" the chair creaked beneath him.

"When did we start making only those promises we can keep?" I asked him in amazement. "That was her condition. Otherwise she wouldn't have agreed."

Haim looked at the pictures spread out on the desk. "Be careful not to get too close," he said suddenly. His voice sounded as if it came from underground. "Keep your soul, your lust, out of it."

"You always say to work with the soul," I told him. "That it's impossible to carry out a mission when we're remote. That the separation between body and soul is artificial, the invention of freethinkers."

"With the Arabs we don't have a problem," Haim stretched the bum leg out in front of him. "We're so angry at them we don't have any trouble being brutal. Look what happened to you. You'll never forgive them for fucking up your illusion of peace. When you came to work here, you had a bumper sticker with white clouds in the blue sky and angels hovering among them. Every morning, I'd check in the parking lot to see if you had taken it off. Believe me, the morning I saw the bumper sticker had been peeled off I was awfully sorry for you. Look at her," he pointed to the big black and white picture printed with the forgotten interview, "is she still so beautiful?"

"Yes," I nodded.

Haim hesitated, and said he felt uneasy, that he had a bad feeling. "But I can't replace you now," he muttered to himself. "You're the only one suited to this assignment. Did you call the advisor?" He meant the psychologist the service recommended to workers who went nuts.

"I'll call," I promised.

"You've got to meet him," said Haim. "That's what I promised them for not suspending you." Haim stood up slowly and went back to tend to his important matters.

After the gorgeous picture of the pregnancy, Daphna appeared only at the edges of photos of others. The baby was born at the end of the glory years, when the media traces she left began to fade. To remain famous, you've got to work at it every single day, and to the credit of Daphna and Ignats, let it be said that they apparently stopped trying. I Googled them and found a few items about Avital Ignats, his return to religion; then he vanished. The two films he made could be gotten at any video store.

I spent a lot of time at home in those days. In the evening, I jogged around the neighborhood and did another few kilometers on the shoulder of the freeway. I ate the schnitzel and rice my mother-in-law made. I helped Sigi bathe the child. I read books before going to sleep.

"I have to give them an answer about Boston," Sigi kept saying over and over.

I tried to get close to her, to calm down, to be gentle, but she only wanted to hear that we were going. Boston was waiting, Boston wouldn't wait. Finally I blew up and roared, on one damn night of a heat wave, that I wasn't going, I didn't give in.

A-frame wooden houses were built on the Caesarea dunes. They were too small to live in year round because they had only a lower floor and a triangular roof. In the seventies they were sold as vacation houses on the European model for wealthy city-dwellers from Tel Aviv and Haifa. But the really rich bought villas with swimming pools, a few kilometers from there, and the A-frames were abandoned in time and became deserted wooden skeletons. The sand slowly enveloped them.

The sea was stormy when I arrived. Waves came from afar and broke on the shore. I tripped on tangled fleshy leaves and gigantic ants' nests. Daphna had indicated the A-frame inspired by French summer houses she had bought with Ignats with ready cash when they returned to Israel. There was no sign on the door and an old bike missing a wheel stood outside. The wooden door was worm-eaten and my knocking wasn't answered. In the picture she showed me, the child was sitting in a plastic wading pool on a green lawn, which was now covered with sand.

In the territories, we have a method of getting people out of their holes, there are dogs and there are neighbors and there's tear gas, but here my means were limited and I had come alone. A person has to come out sometime to buy food, or drugs, or to get a breath of air, after all the guy isn't Anne Frank. But I didn't have the patience to wait for him all day. I walked behind the cottage and peeped through the screened window. He wasn't on the ground floor. I stepped up onto a board and it made a loud creak. I hoisted myself a little more, up to the windowsill on the second floor, I knew I'd regret it when I felt a twinge in my back; when I was about to roll inside, I heard a window open above my head. A few centimeters from me was a pale, very thin face, covered with a scraggly beard, the eyes laughing strangely. The hand was holding a big kitchen knife. "Stop!" I yelled, and he retreated a little. His torso was naked. "I won't hurt you," I said, and he withdrew a little more.

"Get out of here," he said in a childish voice, brandishing the knife in an unstable hand.

"I'm getting down now," I said. "Open the door."

"I'll cut you," he said from above.

"You won't cut anybody here. Daphna sent me. I'm a friend," I said from below, as in some kind of perverse serenade.

The door opened slowly, I heard him shuffle back, and he was no longer holding the knife. Inside, as expected, all kinds of things; dozens of books, and dishes had been tossed about, and the place reeked of sour milk.

"Who are you?" he stood in my way. His body was beautiful and long and very thin, and up close I could see in his eyes that he wasn't healthy.

I said I was a friend of Daphna's, that she sent a little money with me, and she wanted me to find out how he was. I gave him the five hundred I had taken out of the agents' petty cash. In Gaza, that sum could have supported a family for a month. Here it would barely be enough to buy him cocaine for one day. Nevertheless, the money softened him. He put it into his shorts' pocket and moved out of my way.

"Let's go outside," I suggested. "There's a nice wind from the sea. It's a little musty here."

"You can go out," he said. "I'm not." His eyes were red. He didn't look at me. His arms were full of holes and scars from shooting up. He noticed my look and pulled a dirty sweatshirt from some chair, and the long sleeves covered his arms.

"You're not a cop, are you?" he asked. "I saw you in the distance, when you came. You made a lot of noise. Except for mice, nobody comes here. It's just like a cop to be so clumsy." He had a childish laugh, and when he laughed his eyes squinted and you could like him.

I promised him I wasn't a cop. I asked what he needed.

"I need money," he said. "What you brought me is a joke."

I cleared off a pile of clothes and God knows what else to sit on an old wooden chair. "That's enough for a nice shopping trip to the supermarket," I said. "There are families who could live on that for a week."

Yotam Ignats laughed until he almost choked. "Mother always finds strange people," he said. "She's great at that. Creatures from the moon. You don't look like a cop, I know cops. I'll bet you're some lousy actor mother sleeps with, who comes to put on an act for me. She's got no money for private investigators so she sends me fakes. I know because I took everything she had, my poor mother. You passed my audition, congratulations." He clapped his hands and stamped his feet and split his sides laughing.

"You're in a good mood," I said.

"I bought some good stuff." He crossed his legs and folded up in himself, as if he were freezing. "I met a rich girl, we bought stuff for rich people. For a week I've been living on the leftovers. But it's running out, unfortunately, and I don't think she'll want to see me again. In the end, we had a scene, like in the movies."

He was talking defiantly, in a clear voice in his mother's good language, as if he had been waiting a long time for somebody he could talk to. But my responses didn't interest him, he spoke to hear the sound of his own voice.

I picked up one of the books lying on the floor, something by Jung on Job, in English. "Interesting?" I asked.

"It's my father's, all of it. He left it here," said Yotam in a childish voice. "He lived here after he ran away from us, in the sand, like a cave man. Until he went up to Jerusalem and from there he went down into the grave. The books turned his mind to mush. I only have fun with them, killing time. I don't believe in anything people write. Did you read that Jung, hear of him? Probably not . . . "

I asked if he wanted me to help him clean up a little. The smell was becoming unbearable, the little sink was full of old dishes, covered with mold. The tail of at least one mouse passed in front of my eyes. "If you want to, clean up," he said. "I'm not going to get mixed up in that. I'm going upstairs now, with your permission, all of a sudden, I don't feel so good. You disturbed me in the middle. I need to sleep a little. Thanks anyway for the money, just tell her to bring more, or else she'll have to buy me a tombstone soon, and I heard there's a shortage of marble. She's got to give me more. As far as I'm concerned, she can sell the apartment, the building is falling apart anyway. Let her come live here, at the sea, the air here is excellent. I'll go away, I want to go to Cuba, that's what I should do. Just lock up . . . "

Yotam went up the creaking stairs, finally breaking away from the conversation. What did they do to him to put him in such a state? I asked myself. I went to the filthy kitchen corner and hesitated a moment. But I promised her to take care of him. I checked whether there was running water in the faucet, and I started washing the dishes, trying not to breathe through my nose; there was weeks of mold on them and cockroaches and filth. I crushed the living insects one by one with a heavy frying pan, then I filled the sink with water and soap and soaked the dishes in it. I recalled something written by some Buddhist sage about how much he enjoyed washing dishes, blessing the dishes and the moment. High waves broke before my eyes in the small window. I'd be willing to open that rotten wooden house to them, for them to wash away all the filth. I stood at the sink a long time. When I finished, I felt dizzy and sat down on a chair, I picked up the Jung book, leafed through it a little, my eyes grew heavy, and a slumber descended on me. When I woke up, it was dark in the cottage and still as the grave. I was scared.

I checked to see if my gun was in its place—I didn't know what that junkie was capable of—and went up to see what was going on with him. He was lying on a mattress covered with a filthy, bloodstained sheet, reading. "Hey," he started. "You're still here? You didn't go?"

"I cleaned up your filth downstairs."

"Fantastic," he turned his face to me as he lay there. "You want to do my laundry too? I don't have even one clean tie . . . "

I bent over him and thrust my head into his face. "I'm here only because of your mother, you little shit"—the Buddhist monk didn't last very long—"and now I'll start educating you. I'll clean this hole of every grain of stuff and I'll lock you inside until you clean up. Look at you with all those punctures, in the filth." He groped for the knife left under the window. I stepped on his hand, trying not to hurt him too much.

"What is wrong with you?" I yelled. "What are you going through?"

Now he laughed non-stop, and the laughter gradually turned into the wailing of a wounded animal. "Do you know how many people Mother sent to help me? Do you know how many psychiatrists, neurologists, philosophers, jerks, have been here? Poor Mother, God almighty, how many professors she had to sleep with to make them agree to make a house call to me . . . Oh, you make me laugh, you make me cry. Have you got a little bit of stuff by chance?"

Yotam lay with his arms spread to the sides, pale, thin as a skeleton, punctured. "Shoot me," he said. "I saw your gun. Nobody will know, mother will think Azariya whacked me, do it already . . . "

"Who is Azariya?" I asked.

Suddenly a sober and focused look pierced the junkie's mask. "Hey, you're not one of Mother's poets," he said. "They're all stupid wimps. Maybe you really are a private detective, but they're pretty miserable too. You're from someplace else, wonder where mother found you. You've got to watch out for my mother. Run away from her as long as you can."

He was darker than she was, but looked very much like her with his height and long limbs. How come she didn't come and take the needles out of his veins, sit with him day and night and make sure he didn't hurt himself?

"Nukhi Azariya, that's the man who's chasing me," he said. "He thinks I stole a kilo of stuff from him. Fine white powder, like baking powder for making challahs in the synagogue. I'm not taking the blame for it. He's demanding fifty thousand dollars. Great guy, an officer in the Golani Brigade, BA in management from the Open University, high class person. Very good man. I'm waiting for him to find me here and destroy me."

"Where can I find him?" I asked.

"At home, I think," he said. Now he was talking feverishly and quickly, as if some fire had been lit in him. "He's a homebody. Before we fell out, I used to go to his house a lot. He loves culture. I'm the only one who could talk with him. He's surrounded by all sorts of underground apes, very low class people. I brought him books. Here, Yotam, buy some books for yourself, but also buy me something good. Only serious things.

Aristotle, Machiavelli, Shakespeare, all that. He really enjoyed them, that Nukhi. Extraordinary guy, as Mother likes to say. A very intelligent man. He's also got a terrific wife, a Dutch woman. He found her when he set up the network in Amsterdam. The most sensitive woman I've ever seen. She's crazy about him, about Nukhi Azariya. He's got an enormous farm in a village. And horses. Jeeps. And he's searching for me."

I knew the village he was talking about, not far from Rehovoth.

"I'm rotting here," said Yotam and blew his nose. "I'm like one of those crabs that hide in the sand. I can't go back to the city. Every street is full of his people, you can't move an inch without them getting onto you."

I promised I'd go talk to Nukhi Azariya for him. "Are you hungry?" I asked. "From the state of the refrigerator, it looks like you haven't eaten in months."

His eyes were blinded by the bare bulb hanging overhead. Now he stumbled again, as if the air had gone out of him, and almost blended with the filthy bed. We sought one another from afar, my eyes were also red and tired, and we were silent.

"I'll bring you food," I said at last, and went downstairs. I drove to the mall, filled a cart with groceries, and added a pack of cigarettes. When I returned, he was lying in the dark upstairs. I made sure he was breathing, put the things in the small refrigerator, wrote my number on a sheet of paper for him to call if he wanted. I hoped I had fulfilled my obligation with that fellow.

"How's the patient from Gaza?"

The head of the ward met me early in the morning before rounds. A weary doctor on night duty in green scrubs came out of the office, having made his report on those who had died during the night.

"Very sick," said the head of the ward. "He won't last longer than a month or two. We can only ease his pain, not cure him. If he had come six months ago, maybe we could have done something for him. Now it's too late."

"What's wrong with him?"

"Pancreatic cancer. A fatal tumor and very painful. The last thing you want to get."

"We need to keep him alive at least for another month," I said.

The head of the ward chuckled. He was a good-looking man, with harsh blue eyes. "Maybe you should have let him in before, that could have helped."

I sought an excuse. "That doesn't depend on me," I said.

"So who does it depend on?" he asked quietly, as if he were amused. "I thought you were lords of life and death."

"I'm just . . . "

"A little cog," the head of the ward completed my sentence and sighed.

He put on his white lab coat and prepared for rounds.

"Without us, he would have died," I tried to persuade him. His sympathy was important to me. "Nobody would have let him in. He was dying in Gaza. We're not to blame for the situation they brought on themselves. I'm not to blame that their leaders stole all the billions we gave them. They could have built a nice hospital with that."

"That's debatable," said the doctor, as he stood before a small mirror on the wall and adjusted the knot in his silk tie. "What do you want from us?"

"Doctor . . . "

"He doesn't look like somebody who could drag a bomb around on himself," said the doctor. "I heard he's a poet. What can he give you?"

"Not a bad poet, by the way," I said. "If you like, I'll bring you his book. He translated himself into Hebrew."

"I doubt I'll get to it, I'm very busy," said the head of the ward, and opened the door on the way to morning rounds. "But maybe my wife will want it. She's interested in poetry."

"Can he get out of here on his own, Doctor?" I asked. That, indeed, was the important thing.

"We'll tranquilize him for a few days, numb his pains, maybe then he can get out for a few weeks, until the end comes. We'll give him a lot of morphine. I hope you don't intend to put him in your cellars, that's not a treatment I'd recommend for him in his condition."

I swallowed his comments in silence, I needed his cooperation. In other places, they would have put the distinguished doctor in his place immediately. "Can I see him now?" I asked.

"He's sedated, we're doing tests on him," answered the doctor and hurried forward. "Tomorrow or the day after, he'll wake up. By the way, he had a visitor today who seemed quite close to him. A beautiful woman. Now if you'll allow me . . . "

I watched him through the window overlooking the ICU. On both sides of him lay elderly and shriveled up patients, their eyes shut and tubes stuck into orifices. They looked completely dead. I really wanted to do them a favor and remove them from that suffering. Hani lay among them, very thin; his face was tormented, but he still looked alive. You'll recover, I said to him in my heart. Don't fade again, I need you.

Sigi announced that she was going to Boston in two weeks. The director of the company demanded an immediate answer from her. It's really an opportunity that won't come again, she explained. The child had to start a new kindergarten there, and she wanted to give him enough time to get adjusted.

"I can't go in two weeks," I said.

"Why not?" she asked. "They won't give you a year off?"

"I'm in the middle of things," I said. "I'm not playing games."

We were sitting in the kitchen. Sigi made a little snack—it was always something little with her—and the child was asleep in bed. Everything's in your hands, I said to myself, this can still be saved. But the blood began rising to my head, I couldn't control it. I was awfully mad at her for taking the child, for demanding I leave, for her silence, for not pleading.

"Maybe you'll leave the child here," I suggested. "You go."

"And who will take care of him? You'll take him to work with you?"

I watched her cutting vegetables for salad in straight, even lines, biting her lips, and I felt a heavy weariness come over me, like sudden inebriation, though I hadn't had anything to drink. I no longer had the strength to say anything.

She brought the bowl and two plates and two slices of bread to the table, sat down, and started crying. "I don't want to go without you, but I have no choice. For a long time now, you haven't been with us. You're in a bad movie."

I looked at her as if from a distance. Nothing penetrated me. "Stop it, you don't have to cry." A fleeting stroke of her hair, more than that I couldn't give her.

"You fight everybody," she went on crying. "There isn't one person in the world you can call friend. They all disappeared. Didn't you notice?"

That's more or less true, I said to myself. But what choice does a person have in this world?

"Are you ready at long last to talk to me?" she said.

I had an attack of hysterical laughter. Sigi looked at me with wide-open eyes, scared, and then vanished into her room. Suddenly I was scared, but I stayed alone at the table until the bleats of laughter turned into a choking cough. I had trouble breathing. I stood under scalding hot water in the shower to calm down—everything was shrouded in steam, I had made a private Turkish bath for myself—and I tried to look at everything from a distance. My eyes closed, thinking died down, I barely got out of there. I was on the verge of fainting. Late at night, I went into the room to appease Sigi, who lay for hours with her eyes open and looked into the dark.

"That's why we don't have any more children," she said. "You can't make children under such awful pressure, nature doesn't allow them to come into such a life," and then I said ugly things to her that I regretted as soon as they came out of my mouth.

I slept on the sofa in the living room and all night long I walked again and again across a bridge suspended over the road leading to the Temple Mount, with its mosques, between knives and hateful looks, and when I came to wash my face in a small fountain studded with turquoise, under a blinding sun, hands were laid on me and I knew they would now slice me to pieces.

Daphna wanted to meet with me urgently, she suggested a coffee shop not far from her house.

The doctor gave me a verbal update: my man was slowly being weaned off the respirator; tomorrow or the day after, he'd be able to talk.

I was a few minutes late because of the parking, because I didn't want to attract attention and park on the sidewalk. The place was almost full. What do they live on, all those people who sit here in the middle of the morning? I asked myself. They're all dressed sharp, as if they were in Milan. She was wearing a dress and had sunglasses on, and for the first time I saw her legs, which I could only imagine before, and they were long and beautiful. We sat outside, on the spacious balcony; the air flowed pleasantly from the sea, and the street looked calm and quiet, as if a disaster was waiting to happen.

"How are you?" she smiled from behind dark glasses.

I ordered café au lait and cake. Daphna finished a tall glass of iced coffee. A delivery boy in the uniform of a mineral water company came along the street and gave her a piercing look.

We're indescribably exposed here, I said to myself. But who are we hiding from? And who knows me? None of my regular clients will suddenly pass by in north Tel Aviv in the middle of the morning.

"Yotam called," she said. "He told me you came to him. He said you're strange. That you looked like you were in disguise. Hard to fool him . . . "

"I tried to help, I bought him food," I said. "He's in an awful state. If my son were in such a state, I'd put him in a locked room and detox him, no matter how much he screamed."

"You're preaching morality to me?" she asked quietly and crossed her legs.

I drank the coffee. She asked how old my child was. I didn't want to let her into my personal life. "Four," I blurted out in torment.

Somebody called to her and she waved to him briefly. Then she took a deep breath, and said: "Something was wrong with him from the start. He didn't stop crying, I didn't sleep for months because of him. I walked around the streets like a zombie, with him in a buggy, at dawn, in the middle of a heat wave, in the afternoon . . . afterward, people asked how I stopped writing. They didn't find any problem with him. Only one doctor who seemed smarter than the others said the child was very sensitive, there are children like that, everything makes him cry. I took that as a dreadful prophecy. He told me to be harsh with him, to give him a Spartan education, not to go to him at night when he cried, not to hold him too much, I wanted to save him, so that's what I did . . . "

What a shame for the child, I thought, I recalled her glowing pictures, she should have hugged him all the time.

"And that doctor was, of course, a criminal, but at that time, it sounded right. He gave me as an example the children of aristocrats in England, those little lords, and the kibbutz where all their children come out as fighter pilots or commandos. I wanted him to be strong and solid, not a poet . . . I was so stupid. Finally he stopped crying. Nobody went to him. How much I want to hold him today, hug him."

"Where was the father?" I asked. I had the impression she was continually greeting people, that the whole coffee shop revolved around her with secret hints. I felt uncomfortable with that.

"The father . . . " Her fingers slowly roved from the plank at one end of the little table to the other. "If you mean Ignats, he really wasn't with us. For two years he sat on a chaise longue on the balcony, smoked, read passionately, looked at the sky, let himself go, wrote notes and didn't let anyone see them. After the second film failed, he had a serious breakdown. By the time the child was born, he was under the influence of his Tsaddik. He did everything thoroughly, from inside, strongly, not to make an impression, absolutely not. Afterward, we stopped seeing him. He was swallowed up in some alley in Jerusalem. When I gave birth, he came to the hospital for ten minutes and disappeared. You must know, after all, you know everything."

"He never came back?" I asked.

"He came back at the end," she said. "After the child grew up. He came broken, came to get food and a place to sleep. He knocked on my door instead of going to the soup kitchen. No teeth, rotten inside, sick, when I caught him sending Yotam to buy him drugs, I threw him out. Afterward, he wound up in Germany, they wrote about him in the paper that he was rehabilitated, that he was making a film on the Holocaust, that the Germans were subsidizing him, that he got married there, oh . . . "

Daphna took off her sunglasses and looked into my eyes. Hers were wet. "I must seem absolutely nuts," she said.

I thought of myself, and my wife who was leaving me and taking the child next week, and about the things I do in my life, and I shook my head, no. For a moment, I forgot what I wanted from her, and where I was supposed to lead the conversation, and she fell silent too. We were just sitting on a hot day on the balcony of a café. Wild basil grew in a planter next to us. I'd gladly drink a shot of whiskey now and end the day before it started.

An acquaintance of hers passed by us, stopped to say hello, Daphna introduced me by my first name, and said we were working on something together for the internet.

"Why did you have to say that?" I asked after the friend had gone off.

"We need a cover, don't we?" she laughed and her laugh scared me. "We're plotting something. Didn't you ever read *Macbeth*?"

"Why did you call me?" I asked. Our sitting in public, on the balcony, in front of the whole city, had suddenly turned scandalous. I had to bring things between us back on track.

"I wanted to thank you," she said frankly. "I was with Hani at the hospital. I saw how nicely they're treating him there. They said the cancer had spread and there's no chance he'll be cured. At least he won't suffer too much, they're filling him with morphine there. I hope they'll let him out for a few days. It's been several years since Hani was last in Tel Aviv."

"How did you meet him?" I asked.

"Do you record all our conversations?" she asked quietly and leaned over to me. Her hair grazed my cheek for a split second.

"Stop," I asked.

"He was walking around here in the late seventies," said Daphna. "I don't even remember how he came. He was part of the group. The only Arab we knew who wasn't a garbage man or an intelligence officer. He was an attraction. And charming. A very sensitive and special person. There were times when he lived in our house, especially after Avital left. He helped me take care of Yotam. It's awfully hard to see him like that. You want to tell me what you want from him? He's on his last legs, how can he help you?"

From inside the café, through the window pane, somebody was looking at us. He was very slowly drinking a beer and looking at us non-stop. "Do you know that man?"

"I know him," she said and both of us suddenly became uneasy and the air around us was blazing hot. "As I know most people here. I was born here. This is my neighborhood. I have barely left it, through all my metamorphoses."

The man stopped looking at us. Next time we wouldn't meet in such an exposed place. I asked for the check.

"I want to help him," I said. "Believe me."

"Suddenly that Arab touches your heart more than the others?" her laugh lit up the table for a split second, even swept me up. We laughed so hard people around looked at us.

"For some reason, I trust you," she said quickly. I got up and followed her dress in the line of shade of the street. "And I'm not sure that's good for you. I see something hidden in you. Eyes of a poet, the *etrog* dealer, you're not a simple person. Yotam also thought there was something strange about you. Interesting what Hani will think of you. I won't let you touch him, you hear?"

Her face revolved around me all day. I held onto the line of her raised cheek to recall her. And began yearning for her.

I finally had to meet with the advisor. "If you don't go to him," said Haim, "they'll never let you back into interrogations."

The advisor was a tall, athletic man with gray hair, who greeted me in sandals in his clinic at Kibbutz Shefayim. From the lawn outside wafted an afternoon calm, the distant voices of children. The glow of the setting sun fell through treetops heavy with foliage. I would have preferred to talk with a woman. Quietly, without much introduction, he asked me to tell him about the work, the pressures, what happened. I gave him as precise a description as I could.

"What did you feel?" he asked.

I recalled the last look of the fat man who choked, who knew his end was near, how I respected him for not talking. "I wasn't mad at him," I said to the therapist. "I understood him. It was something mechanical, to get the secret out of him, the way you get a tumor out of somebody. With pliers, with a white hot blade, hanging by the feet so the secret will fall out of his head. We hated the Inquisition, but they knew how to get the job done. They simply extracted the confession as a dentist takes out a rotten tooth." I knew those words wouldn't help me get back to the job, but it relieved me a little to get them out. "How do they expect you to stop a suicide bomber," I said to him. An orange sun poured in through the screened window. "Reason alone doesn't work. Reason has no place in their work, and it has no place in ours. We are two tribes of gorillas hitting one another. Like Kubrick's *2001: A Space Odyssey*, only our sticks are more advanced. We use spy satellites to smell the belch from the mouth of some guy in Jenin after his meal of hummus with beans and onions. In the end, it comes down to pain, skin, nerves, the stinking bag, the hands in cuffs that bite into the flesh. To keep you from having to use that, they have to be deathly afraid of what you're liable to do to them. But they're not scared enough. They've heard about all the kinds of torture we can't employ. So now and then you've got to do something out of the ordinary, brutal, so the rumor will spread. I had no problem with the second one, the greasy-haired pimp, the one whose teeth I knocked out. I had no respect for him. Because of people like him, they're losing. But the first one, the fat one, he was a strong man. He didn't care if he died. He was not going to fold or to betray. He knew he had to gain time, another few hours, until his little brother blew himself up. He wanted to die with him. They build monuments to people like that."

I went on like that for a long time, without stopping, running off at the mouth, at times I forgot the therapist was there. He was silent and wrote. It was nice to sit in his room and get out words from the heart.

When I fell silent, he asked only one question: "Do you want to continue doing what you do?"

So the cat was out of the bag. I thought he wanted to hear me, to treat me, but all at once, he moved over to their side. Everything I said would go to them, there would be no immunity here.

"They want me to stop?" I asked.

"What do you want?" he asked. All his questions were open—not like with us, we demanded places, dates, names.

"I want them not to kill us," I said.

"And you, do you want to live?"

I didn't hold back. I described my recurring dream—Temple Mount, the turquoise faucets, my slaughter—and he smiled for the first time, couldn't repress the smile, as if he had come upon the elephant man of psychology. "That's where the binding of Isaac was, right there," he whispered in amazement, and leaned back satisfied as if he had just finished screwing.

Doctor Freud didn't ask a thing about my wife, the child, my parents, Rehovoth. I would have gone into all that if he had asked, I wanted to talk with somebody. He didn't ask.

I asked when to come back. He said it wasn't urgent, but he recommended resting a little more. I was sorry about what I had said, that I was furious, that I didn't behave with restraint. Who was he anyway? A stranger who works for them. You can never be sorry for silence, only for chatter.

I drove to Ikhilov Hospital in the midst of the evening rush hour, past the towers on the banks of the Ayalon Freeway, between the street lights, and I thought how all that electricity damaged us, and we're in a bad way if we send the people who are obliged to be harsher than others to psychiatrists.

I caught the doctor as he was leaving, on the way to his private clinic. He had enough time to tell me they had brought Hani out of the coma; all the tests were done; he had a metastasized tumor that would kill him soon, but he might have a few weeks left to live. From a medical perspective, he could soon be discharged from the hospital, if there was someplace he could rest. "Don't send him back to Gaza," he requested. "There they won't give him medicines and he'll die in awful pain. You can go see him now," he chuckled. "Just leave the pliers outside."

"No," I said. "I don't want to disturb him now. And I'd drop the jokes."

"A spy without humor," he blurted out. "Too bad." Before he took off elegantly for his lucrative evening occupations, he stopped and looked back. "His girlfriend was here again. A very impressive woman. They're close. Maybe he can stay with her a few days."

"Thanks," I said. "Thanks for everything, doctor." My plans were spread out for the whole world to see. Everything happened at its own pace, as if an internal motor was guiding things, without any outside interference, and instead of moving the plot along, I became its instrument.

Daphna announced on the phone that she would take Hani to her place; she arranged for a bed and medical supplies. Everything's going well, I said to myself, with no effort on my part.

"Tomorrow I'm coming to you for a lesson," I said smugly. "The *etrog* man is progressing well."

There was a brief silence, and then she said: "I don't think tomorrow will be convenient. Tomorrow I'll be busy with Hani."

"Then I'll come the day after tomorrow, in the morning," I

said. I stood at the entrance to the hospital, the halt and the lame passing by me.

"I'll call you," she said coldly. "I don't think it'll work this week."

"We've got an agreement, Daphna," I said quietly.

"We had an agreement about Yotam," she said firmly. "And I don't see that you're keeping to it. He's still stuck there in Caesarea, and they still want to kill him, the thugs come to me every day. That's not what we agreed. I thought you had more power."

"I told you I'd take care of that, but the two things have nothing to do with one another."

"There aren't two things," she burst out. The sidewalk on King David Boulevard was covered with red flowers falling from the trees. "There's only one thing. One whole. One deal. Go to Yotam now, then talk with me. I'm not willing to talk about any lessons before you take care of Yotam." And she pressed the mute button, instead of slamming down the receiver with all her might.

The child was sleeping at my mother-in-law's that night, because Sigi had meetings and preparations for the trip. I meant to go to her, read the child a story and put him to bed. I told her I couldn't come, something had come up. Anyway, I felt we had already separated, and it tore me up inside.

"We shouldn't walk around outside? Somebody's going to blow himself up?" asked my good mother-in-law anxiously.

"Maybe somebody is going to blow himself up," I said. "But I don't know much about it." I calmed her. She was still fond of me, or perhaps she hadn't really had any expectations from the start.

The sea at Caesarea was very quiet this time, and the area of the A-frame was silent. Hungry mosquitoes stung me on every exposed strip of skin, on my arms, my neck, my forehead. I had no strength to climb to the window above his bed, so I shouted to him from outside to open up. After a few minutes of shouting, the door opened. I went in, there was a murky light. I didn't see anybody. I climbed the stairs to the second floor and saw that his filthy bed was empty. I turned around and saw his mouth gaping open to the depths of the maw; he was waving a big knife. I was so scared I wanted to kill him.

"I could have slaughtered you like a pig, look how scared you are." He was shaking with laughter, his hair was scattered on his face—his arm moved up and down, cutting the air.

My gun was in my hand, aimed at him. The last time I took it out of its holster was four years ago, at a meeting with a source who looked as if he had flipped. "I'll shoot, Yotam, put that down," I said quietly, and opened the safety catch. "Let's spare your mother one grief at least." He lost his confidence, the ecstatic laughter stopped, the hand came down very slowly, and he landed on the bed weakly, like a man who lost a battle and signals his surrender with an obsequious gesture. I put the safety catch on and thrust the short barrel into his cheek until it hurt and then I put it back in the holster.

"I'm here only because of your mother," I said. "The next time I'll shoot you without thinking twice. Now let's search this place. I'm going to throw out all the drugs." He whined like a child, pleaded with me not to touch anything, but I had already started going through the drawers, looking under the mattress and behind the books. I signaled to him not to move. I removed at least three small plastic bags full of powder and pills from behind the books. Then I went to the tiny bathroom where I confiscated the boxes of Ritalin and the antipsychotic medicines—here and there I scanned the consumer pamphlet out of curiosity—and then went down to the first floor and made a few finds there, too.

"Now, come with me," I said, and grabbed him by the scruff of the neck. He was wearing only his underwear; I told him to put something on, and went out to the sea with him, hand in hand. There were a few cars there leaving the beach at the end of a long day, the children must have been put in the back seat, dead tired, and the parents looked at us like we were a homosexual couple gone nuts, I and my druggy toy boy. Everything was out in the open.

I performed a premature version of the New Year's rite of Tashlikh, throwing out sins, at the shore. He wailed when he saw his treasure thrown into the sea. I shook out the bags carefully so nothing would remain, and then I sat down next to him on the sand. The lights on the chimneys of the electric company glowed above us with the stars.

"I'll kill you when you're not looking," he muttered with his head between his knees. "Everybody can be surprised. Even you. From behind."

"You won't succeed," I said. "You're a junkie and your senses are fucked up. Your reaction times are shot. Your nervous system is gone."

He lay back, his hair was filled with sand. Small waves broke loudly on the shore. Far from us, stood the silhouette of a solitary little tent with a small bonfire burning next to it.

"You really want to get clean?" I asked.

"No," answered Yotam, his enormous face toward the sky. "There's nothing bad about drugs. The problem is money. People are just brainwashed. There are millionaires who snort cocaine all their life. Without stuff they wouldn't get anywhere. Reality is too hard to face without help. The problem is money, capitalism, they don't want little people to use it. Who will be their slaves if everybody's high?"

"You don't really believe that crap," I said. "Look at you, twenty-three years old, you're barely alive."

"They're chasing me," he said. "They won't let me breathe." He asked for a cigarette.

"I don't have a cigarette. I'm here only because of your mother. Fuck up your life by yourself, you're not my son." I thought how Haim would have acted in my place, about his *kippa* and his eastern amiability and the Jerusalem-style wisdom of life and all that, how he would have taken care of him.

"With a father like you . . . " The crooked laugh started climbing onto his face again. "Tell me, did you screw her yet, or does she pay you with money? She doesn't have any money, I don't think she can . . . Did you read her books? Did you see what great sex parts there are? When I was twelve, I found them in a closet. I love to read books. I was a wunderkind, in kindergarten I could already read, did she tell you? You know how it is for a kid to masturbate to passages his own mother wrote? Don't think I read the books from start to finish, between us, they're pretty shitty, but the parts of screwing, there I found . . . "

I stood up to leave him. Behind us were the lights of the concrete bloc called Israel, next to us was the big power station, only in front, in the sea, were darkness and quiet.

"And your father?" I called to him from the distance.

"Ha, the genius," he laughed. He stood up and started running wild like a marionette out of control, throwing his limbs to the sides. "Fellini, Bergman, Karl Marx, Rabbi Nachman of Bratslav, all in one . . . I'm out of control, so forgive me, you threw away what I had left in life. Mother sent you to kill me. In the end, he went back to Jerusalem, the saint, sat in a wheelchair with a stroke, even his Russian woman left him. Those Hassids kept him imprisoned, he couldn't even toss God to hell anymore, poor rag. How arrogant he was, he was the only one who knew everything. He always said everyone envied him, everyone was obsessed with him. What great films he made, two and a half people saw them in the Paris Cinema and even they wanted their money back. Avital Ignats, what a splendid name. But by the time I was six months old, he wasn't there anymore. He wanted me to come to him a few years ago. Where's my son? I miss him. What did I find there? A broken vessel. He thought he was the patriarch Isaac, he put his hand on my head. I expected him to ask for forgiveness. Where were you all the time, Father? Where were you? He didn't understand what I said to him. I tried to talk about Nietzsche. I read the books he had left, I tried to impress him. But he sat and drooled. The man was totally wiped out. I ran away from there . . . " Yotam dropped onto the sand and started shaking.

For a moment, I touched his shirt, which was wet with sweat and spray from the waves. His eyes were shut. Everything was dripping down from him, soon he would melt into the sand like a jellyfish.

"What happened with that Nukhi Azariya?" I asked. "How did you get mixed up with him?"

"Who are you anyway?" he whispered under the noise of the waves. "Why should I tell you?"

He's tied up tighter than the people in our cellars, I thought. They've at least got something in their head that sustains them: hope, children, desire for revenge. With him there's nothing, he's got handcuffs on his brain that press inside and distort everything, from the moment he was born . . .

"Let's say," he began hesitantly, then coughed. I helped him take off the wet shirt. "Let's say there's somebody who lived in New York and dreamed of doing something there. Making powerful movies, like Scorsese, *Taxi Driver*. His mother paid for him to study in the best film school, he doesn't know where she dug up the money for that. But he doesn't have money for other things—for instance the stuff he takes and without which he can't concentrate; he never was any good at school. He lives in a hole, a single room he shares with rats. Then some Israeli comes to him in some café where he sits, talks with him . . . You don't get me, right?"

"No, anyway you can't hear anything in this wind."

"And that Israeli . . . " Yotam coughed. "He invites him to eat in a fancy place, brings along some girls, one who looks just like Jennifer Lopez. And this is a fellow who, if he had stayed in Israel would never have had anything to with a man like that. The two of them would have gotten to the grave without sitting down and drinking coffee with one another. But in New York it's different, and before you part, he tells you he's got an empty apartment. In Trump Tower, on the river. He gives you the key, and one of the Mexican women goes there with you in a cab at his expense. You start feeling like a human being, at long last, you've got experiences you can put into a film, and you're in America, America! tasting the good life of America. And it's an amazing apartment with a view of the whole city, and the doorman knows you're coming and greets you, everything's arranged, your head is spinning, and he makes sure to put in your pocket the sweetest stuff you ever tasted, something that just came from Pedro's field in Colombia . . . "

"That was Azariya?" I asked.

High tide sent little waves onto the shore, wetting the sand under his feet. I pulled him back, he was light as a child. Yotam nodded and said: "The most generous human being I ever met. He didn't ask me anything about Ignats, hadn't seen his films, didn't read my mother's books. Said he was discharged from the Golani Brigade from a village in the south, that he went to New York and met some people, and started doing business there. Oh, it's getting cold here . . . "

I took off my shirt and sat in my white short-sleeved undershirt. I put it on him.

"And he was happy for me. I told him about the film I wanted to make, and he said he'd give me money for it. And suddenly came wild energy, I had everything going for me, and then came Christmas and he bought me tickets and sent me home to Israel for a vacation."

I recalled a fellow they once brought us from Allenby Bridge with a stomachache and a guilty face. We thought he was smuggling notes with instructions for an attack, but after two hours on the pot, two kilos of heroin in cellophane bags came out of him, like a stuffed sausage.

"With a suitcase," said Yotam. Now I saw only his silhouette, he sat wrapped up in my shirt, feverish and talking. "I put my clothes in it, and books, and a present for Mother. I really didn't know what he had put in there. He apparently hid it in the sides. Nukhi sat with me all night before the flight, we went out together, we talked about the future. He made sure I got onto the flight clean, only with tranquilizers, that I didn't make a bad impression at Ben-Gurion Airport. I got through customs calmly, those fat guys sit there and don't stop anybody—I went through the green line like a big shot. Mother was waiting for me among all the Orthodox Jews, kisses and hugs. How good you look, what a beautiful suitcase. Come on, Mother, let's go. I was afraid of those dogs you sometimes see at airports, but they don't use them here because they remind people too much of the Nazis . . .

"The next day, somebody met me under Mother's house. We sat in a big van with opaque windows, and he took the suitcase, and gave me another one just like it. I went back to New York, back to Paradise. Nukhi supplied everything I needed. I left school; Kubrick didn't finish film school either. I was living an excellent movie, I was on top of the world. I started writing a screenplay and gave him every chapter to read when I finished. In the summer he sent me again, with the same suitcase, this time it was a little heavier. And this time too everything was easy, even though I was pretty spaced out when I arrived, but I was used to keeping my cool. Mother, kisses, my nice little room, exchange of suitcases. I escaped after three days, went to Rome for a week, and there I fell into a depression; it was life itself that got me down."

A trio of battle helicopters passed over the sea heading north, pointing spotlights that turned the water white. I looked at that shaking body, the thicket of dirty hair covering the face, and I tried to figure out how far from here you could get in a rowboat.

"Afterward I made a short film," the voice kept coming out of the covered face. "More video art than film. I managed to get it into some festival, they wrote my name in the *Village Voice*. I got a little work on the set of a producer, the first time something good happened to me. I tried to clean up a little, forget all the garbage, forget the crappy Israel, home. I thanked Nukhi, said I was leaving the apartment, thanks a lot for everything. 'Good luck,' he told me. 'All the best. But you owe me one more trip. Just one more.' I tried to get out of it, but he talked about all the money he had spent on me, and how he had gotten me out of the shit at my hardest time. I couldn't argue with him. Just once more, he promised me. The same suitcase, now it was really heavy. I swallowed uppers and downers, Ritalin. I got on that flight, scared, my balls were shaking even at JFK. All the way here, I had horrible dreams, sweating like a pig, and as we landed in Israel, a uniformed policeman got on the plane, walked around here and there; we were all delayed until he finished. I got out of the jetway, went to the baggage claim, and couldn't go on. When the suitcase came, I took it to the bathroom, locked the stall, took all the tags off it, wiped my fingerprints off it, took all my things out of it, stuffed them into bags, threw them into the garbage. The suitcase stayed in the bathroom. I went out to Mother, 'What, no suitcase?' 'No, it got lost, went by mistake to Krakow. Mother, I can't go sleep in your house, there's something I've got to take care of, I'll come in a few days.' That was four months ago. Ever since, I've been running away. They had a lot of stuff in there. A very heavy suitcase. Maybe ten kilos."

Run away, I thought, why do you stay? Run away to the farthest place, start all over there. Forget Ignats and films and all that nonsense. Save your ass.

I sat close to him. Don't be disgusted by him, he came out of his mother's flesh. "I can get you immunity from prosecution," I said. "But you'll have to testify against him."

Yotam laughed, stood up, waved his hands in the air. "You're joking? They'll whack me." And once again, his head dropped and sweat dripped from his face. "I'm crippled, got no strength. I can't deal with them. You're looking at a dead man."

"What about the films?"

"One Ignats making bad films is enough," he giggled, his voice suddenly sounded young and vulnerable. "The world will get along without my films."

"What will save you?" I asked. It was now dark before us, even the distant tent was folded up and the bonfire next to it had collapsed into embers.

"Give me back my stuff." He got down on his knees. "And everything will be all right. Give me only one bag to get through the night. Afterward, I'll make it on my own. Tell Daphna to forget me or to send me money, this talking won't save me . . . "

"I threw it all away," I said. "Nothing's left."

I went on sitting with him for a while. I wasn't in a hurry to get back home. Sigi was organizing for the trip, the whole apartment was full of cartons, the child must be asleep by now. Before I parted from him, I took five hundred shekels out of my pocket and gave it to him. I knew it would make its way to the nearest drug dealer in the Arab village tonight.

I left him on the sand, bound in his own handcuffs. "I'm asking you for only one thing," I said. "Here's a phone card. Call your mother, tell her I was with you. Tell her you feel better."

"For this money, I'm even willing to suck your dick," he said in the voice of a cartoon character. "No problem, boss. I'll talk with her, don't worry. We're friends, right? Sit together at the sea, talk about life. I sat like this with Nukhi Azariya, too. He really liked listening to what I had to say, between one trip and another. Just watch out for the knives. Don't let your guard down, friend, watch your back."

He watched me from below. The lights of the power station picked out the delicate lines of his face. I could have hugged him, I could have kicked him in the face. I turned around and walked away and my shoes sank in the sand.

Hani was sitting on Daphna's seventies sofa, nicely dressed, khaki pants and a checked shirt, very thin, and watching television. From the distance, I could see he was watching Al Jezeera; they had a pretty and mysterious newscaster with great eyes whom I also loved.

I was an uninvited guest, and Daphna was embarrassed. "Come into the living room a moment," she said, and introduced us quickly. "A student," she presented me. "He wants to write a book." For the time being that was enough. I didn't mean to up the ante immediately.

We sat in the kitchen and made a whole production about the *etrog* man, who had now arrived at the isle of Naxos, an earthly paradise, and stayed in a village with a temple to Venus surrounded by olive groves just outside it. Sigi and I had been there on our honeymoon; we escaped on a ferry from the flocks of tourists in Santorini, and I didn't want to leave. "This isn't a bad story," said Daphna. "You might do something with it à la Marguerite Yourcenar." She was tense and I didn't believe her.

She went to Hani and asked if he needed something. I heard him thank her with delicacy: No, he didn't have any more pain, maybe only a little, in a while he'll take the pill and sleep a bit. "In a little while, I'll come sit with you," said Daphna.

"Yotam called," she whispered when she came back to the kitchen; there was a leaky faucet dripping slowly and getting on my nerves. "He said you were at his place. That you helped him a little. He sounded better. That you convinced him to find work. Now you've got to arrange it so he can come back to the city." Her eyes were suddenly enormous, her lips were red and thick; I couldn't say if she was an old woman or a young girl, it wasn't important, because she swallowed me up. I ate the cake I loved, we did a little more with descriptions of the view, and suddenly Hani appeared and stood above us. He moved slowly, and up close he looked very bad, thin and yellow as parchment, but his smile was sad and sweet. "Hey!" Daphna blurted a small shout of fear, as if he had caught us plotting. "How did you get up by yourself?"

"I love that cake," he said. "I smelled it," and the three of us began laughing all at once. "I can eat what I want, I don't have a problem with diet." His Hebrew was slow and precise, like that of a person who learned a foreign language in a cultured way, not with bestial and furtive foreign accents, to survive, but from a longing for education.

Daphna cleared a place for him next to her, I moved my chair a little, she made him strong tea. "It's warm here as in Gaza," he said, and she offered to turn on the air conditioner. "No need," he said. "Inside I'm shivering with cold."

I knew basic facts about him: that he was born in 1948, that he had one son and one daughter, that his wife had died young of an illness. Mainly I knew the conclusion to his Tel Aviv episode, because then there was a tail on him. I preferred not to remember those things now because the man was heartbreaking and pleasant company and the two of us were sitting on either side of Daphna like long-time residents in a boarding house.

"I hope I didn't disturb your lesson," said Hani.

"No, that's just fine, we're about to finish," I said. "I have enough homework."

I had had time to read his old collection of stories, published in Jordan, and filled with yearnings for the Land and the citrus groves and the wells and the old villages, even though the narrator was born in Gaza and had never seen them with his own eyes. It was a frightening book in its emotional force.

"What are you writing about?" asked Hani, and I really

blushed and told him about the *etrog* man, I tried to garner remnants of truth from within to be convincing.

Hani asked why my man was going to the islands, and I explained that the Temple was destroyed and the Land was desolate and they needed to bring *etrogs* for Sukkot.

Daphna reminded him of how they had once sat with a man named Barukh in a Sukkah in Jaffa that had been named in memory of the exodus from Egypt, and Hani said the fellahin would set up huts in the field during the harvest, the whole family would pick crops by day and sleep in the hut at night. Daphna said that appears even in The Song of Solomon, and their conversation was easy and fluent, a chorus of mature voices. He ate a few crumbs of the cake which really was very soft and rich and tasty.

"If Daphna agreed to take you on, you must have talent," said Hani. "She has no patience for dummies. We've been friends for many years now. Most important in writing is not to despair. As in love. It can break your heart in the end, but that's what a person lives for."

"Right," Daphna nodded, and looked charming and calm. I felt I was sitting with wise adults, and I was amazed that they were talking with me at all. Until a professional thought darted through my head, bringing things back to where they belonged, and I felt a stabbing pain in my eyes.

Hani said he was going to lie down now; the doctor had suggested he not exert himself, and the medicine made him foggy. He held my hand strongly, said see you again and looked into my eyes. Death was visible in the depths of his eyes. Then he leaned on Daphna on the way to the sofa she had arranged for him in the living room.

We sat in the kitchen a few more minutes. The role playing was over. I promised her in a whisper to try to sweep the area so Yotam could come back to the city, and we arranged to meet two days later.

Afterward, at home, I sat with Sigi and the child at a silent supper. Most of their things were already in cartons, the house had been turned upside-down, but there was no point commenting. The child scattered rice around the plate and asked why I wasn't coming with them. I answered that it was because of work, but I'd come visit. "Come with us," Sigi said and I explained to her again that I couldn't leave in the middle of an assignment. She smiled to herself and dropped the subject, as if I had finally released her. "Go," I said. "You're right. Don't miss out because of me."

"It's not me I pity," she said. "I'll do just fine, but my heart breaks for the child."

In the archive I found that they had talked properly with Hani only once, in 1982, a few months before the war. At a certain stage, he had drawn attention, walked around the area a lot, and they decided to call him in for a talk. His information had been typed up and whoever talked with him must have retired long ago. Hani said he was a writer, had been writing since his youth. His stories were published in journals in the West Bank and in the Arab world, he focused on short stories and also wrote poems sometimes. He hadn't yet written a novel, for that you needed time and a livelihood.

Who was the intelligent interrogator who went so deeply into his kind of creativity? I wondered. Maybe somebody like me, who for some reason was in the deep freeze?

He went on and recounted how he had been invited a few years before to a meeting of Jewish and Palestinian artists at Tel Aviv University (the interrogator wrote "Palestinian," erased it and wrote "Arab," and erased it again and went back to "Palestinian"). There he met a lot of artists who invited him to stay with them, and then came invitations to other events. There was a nice evening at "Tsavta," where he read his poems and afterward he came often to Tel Aviv. Some of the stories he wrote were translated for the literary supplement of *Ha-aretz*.

Then they asked him specifically about certain names, they wanted him to talk about the political meetings on Jewish-Arab brotherhood he had attended, and he gave all the details. Daphna's name was also mentioned: Hani said he met her at one of the events and stayed at her house now and then. The interrogator didn't go more deeply than that; she was one of many other names.

"In Gaza I work as a translator for the UN," Hani said. "I've got a natural talent for languages. I learned Hebrew when I was young, when I worked with Jews on vacation. I joined my older brothers, who did all kinds of jobs, mainly in Ashkelon." The family was originally from Jaffa. He didn't remember anything from there because he was only a few months old when the war broke out.

When he was interrogated he was thirty-four years old. His face in the picture is pleasant, smooth, not aggressive. Really a good Arab—except for the ironic smile obvious even in the old photo; we don't like smiles like that. It's important to look at a person's face, it's the basic alphabet of the interrogator. And the very next page says he was arrested a few days later for interrogation at the installation in Ashkelon on suspicion of connections with the PLO.

"Why did they arrest him?" I muttered. But I immediately told myself that I wouldn't have acted any different. Something didn't smell right in his story, he sounded like a mole.

The next interrogation was done while he was in detention, and the intensity rose from the page. The sentences were much shorter and written in a barely legible hand. They asked him about trips, once he was in Italy and twice he went to Jordan. In Jordan, he visited relatives; in Italy, he made a tour with his wife. That was the only time they were abroad, they saw Rome and ate macaroni. Perhaps after such an answer, somebody smacked him. They asked about who he knew in Gaza, mentioned forgotten names of junior PLO activists.

A doctor of Arab literature at the Hebrew University put a special expert opinion on Hani's writings in the file, which I found in a shabby plastic bag. He wrote that even though his stories and poems don't preach violence, and the lyrical style is restrained, they throbbed with a sense of injustice and a strong desire to return to the lands that had been taken; that was the leitmotif of his creation, and so may have been a disruptive influence on Arab readers and a demoralizing effect on the Israeli public.

After three days, he was released with no accusation at all, but he was forbidden to re-enter Israel.

They went easy on him, I thought; with such connections he could have easily been arrested for several months. All those associations were exceptional, it smelled bad. The man didn't take care of those bohemians' cars, nor did he serve hummus chips and salad. They forbade him to return to Israel and thus solved the problem. It can plausibly be assumed that they tried to recruit him—that's what they always do—and he didn't agree. That was his punishment.

At the end of the dossier were a few letters from his friends, addressed to politicians, to let him in. They wrote that he was a moderate, a bridge to peace. All of them were filed with brief remarks of refusal written by professionals.

In the afternoon, I took the child to the sea. As we entered the water, the sun was still blinding and strong. His little body floated in a purple inner tube. I taught him to rise above the smooth waves, and after every wave, he shouted with excitement. Hundreds of times. Water sprayed in his eyes, and he heroically refrained from whining. I showed him how I put my whole head into the water and dived without fear.

The water turned purple at sunset, and only when it got dark did he agree to come out. We ate the watermelon Sigi had prepared. The child was shaking under the towel. Go with them, I said to myself, leave the cellars. Not yet, I thought, that won't solve anything. I saw myself sitting on a bench on a foreign street, wrapped in a coat, shaking with cold, under foreign trees dropping their leaves, killing time, growing old. "It was a lot of fun in the sea, Papa," said the child. I took off his bathing suit and dressed him in shorts and a shirt. "Papa, I got tired," he said and I picked him up, along with all the beach things. By the time I put him in his safety seat in the car, he was asleep, covered with salt.

Haim was stuck in his orthopedic chair, behind the long Formica table, his eyes red with the great effort of following the information on the screen. "When's the meeting with the son?" he asked. "Is that organized? Is there a date yet?"

"Not yet," I said. "There's a problem on the way." I told him about the issue with Yotam.

"Splendid family, a scion of great rabbis, philosophers, physicians, how did such a degenerate boy come from that," said Haim angrily.

"Drop it now, Haim, come on," I said impatiently. I knew where the conversation was going, his usual tirade about the loss of values. "I want to get moving on this."

I wanted his advice about how to deal with the drug dealer Nukhi Azariya. Haim suggested I talk with the police, let them take care of it, why should I mess around with that. "The police won't do anything," I said. "I've already talked with them. They know him, they're following him, playing a double game with him. He's also a source of intelligence for them. Five minutes with the intelligence gatherer of the elite central police unit and I understood how deep they're into him. He buys safe documents from them and they can't touch him. How long have you been following him? I asked them. Three or four years. Meanwhile, he's gotten very rich and can hire a battery of lawyers who get him out of any trouble. He's very careful, doesn't get his own hands dirty, only his name hovers overhead."

"What does he want from the boy?" asked Haim.

"Seventy-five thousand dollars," I said. "That's the value of the drugs the kid stole from him, or lost for him, depending what you believe."

I asked Haim for permission to arrest Nukhi Azariya, to scare him so he wouldn't touch the boy again.

"The opposite," said Haim and his finger pressed the keyboard. He never missed anything that appeared on his computer screen, from the synopsis of *Al-Jezeera* editorials to the most sensitive reports from agents. "Do exactly the opposite. You won't manage to scare him. He knows you can't keep him in detention more than twenty-four hours. The Jews have basic laws that guarantee respect for human lives, they were born free to sell drugs. After two hours, you'll have to bring in his defense lawyer. The moment he's released, he'll go looking for your boy to cut off his balls for denouncing him. Don't scare him. Recruit him," said Haim. "Make him a patriot."

Haim is six or seven years older than me, but a hundred times smarter. He's got five children, and a wife who's a social worker with a head scarf, and a lot of peace of mind. He looks like a sweaty post office clerk, but he's a brilliant intelligence officer. Every morning he wakes up at five and manages to study a page of Talmud with a group, and once a week, he gives a lesson in the synagogue.

"When does the wife go?" he asked.

"Tomorrow," I said.

"You mustn't leave her. Finish that business and go," he decreed and went back to looking at the screen.

"You wouldn't let your wife go." I said.

"We cleave to each other," he said. "And my eyes are buried in the ground when a woman approaches. It's a lot harder for you guys. No anchor. I never forbade my wife anything and she didn't forbid me anything. There was no need." In Haim's case, I believed every word that came out of his mouth. The man was a limping and harsh saint. Now and then I was assailed by a burst of love for him. Maybe I needed a father, maybe I needed pity.

I asked Haim if he had an idea of how to get Yotam off drugs. "You won't like what I tell you." His red eyes groped for mine, he squinted slightly. "You know what my answer is."

"Opium for the masses," I said.

"Exactly. The only drug mankind has found to ease its oppression. Faith in the Creator of the World. When he has the courage to shout to heaven and ask for pity and forgiveness, then he'll be cured. That boy has a deep wound in his heart. The pollution of generations, a sediment built up in him, he's a victim, he's not guilty, the poor kid."

"Haim, come on," I said. "His father tried your trick. It didn't help him, he cursed Heaven from the wheelchair in Meah Shearim, imprisoned in his hell."

"He came too late," said Haim. "I remember they wrote about him in the newspapers." The man was a walking trove of knowledge. "He came after Uri Zohar. All of them exaggerate too much."

I asked Haim when he thought I could go back to interrogations. He looked at me, surveyed me, as if he were measuring the structure of my skull. It was a strange moment. And then he said: "I don't know. You still need to go through a process. What you went through was no accident. If you go back now, nothing will happen, the chance will be missed. Aside from that, the psychologist thought you weren't ripe yet."

Somebody creaked open the door, an interrogator I knew well, and Haim gestured to him to wait outside a moment.

"Don't you need me?" I asked. "What did that charlatan write about me?"

Haim got up, limped over to me, put a hand on my shoulder,

and said: "You know how much I love you, but we're getting along without you. Even if an Arab shot you between the eyes, we'd get along, with all our grief. It's a healthy organization. We've got a tradition. Finish this business, be careful not to fall into traps here, go with a commendation to Boston and come back. Live among the goyim a little, it will make you miss us."

When I left, I felt dizzy. I barely said goodbye to the friend who was glad to see me in the corridor. I should have gone home and said goodbye to my wife and child. In a few hours, they were going.

Nukhi Azariya, as the intelligence coordinator of the elite central unit told me, went twice a week to a certain hotel on HaYarkon Street to screw. He gave me the name of the hotel and the time. We sat in a coffee shop on King George Street, one of the last ones that still make *Kremschnitt*, and the policeman devoured three pieces before my eyes. Drunk on sugar and margarine, he came to me and whispered with flashing eyes that they had cameras in the walls. "You won't believe what films we've got from the amazing pussies that shit fucks."

I sat in the lobby half an hour, looked out the big windows at the sea, listened to the French all around me. No one paid attention to me, I could have spent all day there without being bothered. Ever since I had left the interrogations, the announcements, the briefings, the field trips, the daily pressures had all stopped. I was like an entrepreneur who builds an abstract project. I didn't see a single Arab anywhere.

He entered the hotel right on time. The standard compact look of an Israeli man: bouncy walk, close-shaved face, average height, slightly puffed-up muscles, seems to be in good shape, designer jeans and a Lacoste shirt, three bodyguards surrounding him. He went to the counter and got the key. I quickly got up from the soft sofa and approached him at the elevator. I called him by name. The bodyguards immediately went for their guns in their pants, I said to them: "Calm down. I don't have a weapon. I'm a friend. I want to talk with you," I said to him. "I've got a proposition for you."

"I don't know who you are," said Nukhi Azariya. "And I'm not looking for deals with people I don't know." One of his security guards, a man without a trace of Judaism in his face, whispered to me: "Get out of here, or else we'll take you up to the twentieth floor with us and send you flying off the balcony like a bird. Then they'll try to find out what was depressing you. Today they've got post-death psychologists in Abu Kabir."

I hadn't approached him right, I wasn't trained in that line of work. They were usually brought to me packed up and trussed like barbecued chicken; here I had to deal with free people. Azariya was wearing a beautiful delicate gold bracelet. Suddenly I wanted one like that.

"Listen . . . ," I said. But then the elevator came and the muscular cubes shoved me aside and pushed inside. At the last minute, I put a foot across the electronic sensor and went inside. I assumed they wouldn't slaughter me in an elevator in a hotel in the middle of the city, in front of the security cameras.

The apes isolated me in a corner of the elevator, I saw all our skulls in the big mirror overhead, they crushed me hard, but I managed to say: "I'm from the service, Nukhi, and I want to talk to you. I need your help in an important security matter. I'm not from the police, I don't care what your business is. I'm asking you to sit with me for five minutes."

"Leave him alone," said Nukhi. The elevator stopped. They held the door open. "In about two hours, I'll finish freshening up and I'll come down. Then we'll talk."

He strode slowly down the corridor bathed in a soft, delicate light falling through the big windows. His silhouette was reflected on the deserted lawns of Independence Park and on the statue of the seagull with a broken wing and on the breakers in the wonderful sea. Everything was created for this moment of Nukhi Azariya, and at the end of the cool corridor three terrific, slim, smiling Moldovan whores were waiting for him. Everything in the picture was perfect, except me.

I waited downstairs in the lobby for two and a half hours, watching the elevator, deep in thoughts that weren't positive, until Nukhi emerged washed and energetic and surrounded by his thugs. He didn't forget me, walked over to me, dressed elegantly, and suggested we have a late lunch together. "Not here," he said. "I don't touch hotel food." I knew he had a tail all the time, and that now I, too, was part of his police dossier.

What are you doing, dammit? I said to myself, shoved into the black Hummer and looking through slits at the city, like a member of a marine patrol in Baghdad. We went down the slope of the boardwalk, and parked on one of the streets connecting the sea and the Carmel Market. Sigi and I had lived in this area when we were students, we filled a plastic shopping bag in the market every Friday, we felt the tomatoes and chose the freshest arugula. In the afternoon, we went down to the shore, barefoot. Oh, damn the day we moved out of Tel Aviv. One of Azariya's guards set foot on the sidewalk and checked the area, Azariya got out after him, like the king of the world. They ordered me to stay put in the car a few more minutes while they frisked me.

We went into a neglected courtyard full of weeds, walked on a path of worn, rough tiles of one of the little houses still left of Keren Ha-Temanim. On the crumbling wall was a small sign indicating a health center. The man simply can't go from one whore house to another, I said to myself. But as soon as we went inside, I understood that I was wrong, there was a wonderful smell of soap and cleanliness there, and under our feet was a colorful and smooth mosaic, and everything looked welltended and spick and span. An elderly woman in a white smock with a nice foreign smile greeted us, maybe a Turkish woman, maybe Yugoslavian. Nukhi tossed her a hello in a language I didn't recognize, and then said in English that I was coming in with him. She showed us the way to the inside rooms. "I come here once a week," said Nukhi Azariya. "To get clean down to my bones, to open my pores, it purifies the soul. We're the only ones here, don't worry. They close the place for me. Now we strip."

He quickly got out of his clothes. He had a compact and muscular body, maybe a trace too fat, and a healthy prick. I remained clothed. "I'm not talking with you like that, when you're dressed," he said, and covered his loins with a big white towel.

"Where are we going?" I asked.

He laughed. "You're a real coward, come on already."

Nukhi Azariya and I sat next to one another in a wet Turkish bath, sweating down to our bones, in steam and in a dim light. Smells of lilac all around, stringed instruments playing softly in the background, an oud or a bouzouki. An invisible hand brought in a tray with lemonade and cut, ripe, very sweet fruit.

"Drink," he said. "You've got to keep drinking."

"I didn't know there was such a place in Israel," I said.

He had the face of a wild animal, open, calm. His jaw dropped like that of a lion before assailing its prey. I could have put a bullet in him without batting an eyelid, but at the moment I needed something from him.

"Who are you?" he asked.

I introduced myself as much as I could. He looked at every movement of my face, I was going through his internal lie detector.

"You know I was an officer in the Golani Brigade?" he asked slowly and poured cold water on his head. "We'd go with your guys to meetings. We went to Lebanon in your Mercedes. There I learned everything I know. I made the first contacts there. The army was a good school for me. I believe you. You don't look like a cop."

The body emptied its liquids and I put them back, drinking and eating slices of watermelon.

"Sometimes I bring the girls from the hotel here," said Nukhi Azariya. "But today I gave them up for you. This is my day to spoil myself. One day a week for me. What do we live for if not that. Ten years I worked day and night, I put myself in danger, to get to this. Now I can rest a little."

With all the background I had gathered on him, I would have been fully justified if I had attacked him and slammed his head against the beautiful tiles that were rough to the touch. Instead, I was feeling great, like a man among men and even my prick started standing up under the towel.

"Join me here whenever you want," he said. "You've got carte blanche. The next time, we'll bring the girls."

"Why are you offering me this?" I asked, and poured cold water on my head.

"Because I identify people by their face, and you've got a special look," said Nukhi Azariya who leaned on the wall across from me, gleaming with liquids. "You don't want money from me. You don't want a bribe. You look like a person who isn't capable of betraying, I admire people like you."

Apparently my face gave me away because Nukhi laughed. "Of course you can betray, don't insult me, everybody betrays when they have to. All those wise men who talk about the Holocaust, see what they'd do when a Jewish friend came to hide in their house. The decent law-abiding citizen would give him away at once, for fear he'd be caught. Only the criminal, somebody who doesn't give a damn about the law, might hide him. Maybe . . . "

The invisible hand put down a bowl of little kebabs with pine nuts, and very cold beer brewed by monks in Belgium from an ancient recipe. From one moment to the next, it got better. I forgot my whole agenda. I drank the beer calmly and ate the meat with my hands. And when the bowl was empty, he lay on the bare floor, took off the towel and asked: "What do you want from me, my friend?"

"I want you to let Yotam Ignats back into the city," I said.

"Yotam Ignats," he smiled with his eyes shut. "A really interesting guy. I met him in New York. Very educated and brilliant. A pleasure to talk with him. At first, he looked down on me until I started spoiling him. He was bought, too, like everybody else. Did he explain the source of his obligation?"

"He lost a package for you," I said. My head was now heavy from all the food and drink, not to mention the steam.

"That's the problem with junkies," said Nukhi Azariya. "You can't believe a word they say. Look at my arms, smooth as a baby's. Check my nostrils, everything there is also fine. The minute you start to stab yourself, when you've crossed that boundary of the body, everything's broken. Truth and lies no longer have any meaning. He's lying, you know. There was no package."

"Nukhi, I won't get into that . . . ," I cut him off.

"No, my brother, it's important to me that you know the guy is lying. There was no package. I gave him a lot of money to make a short film, I believed him. I thought we were friends, he charmed me. I gave him a hundred thousand dollars to finish his creation. And he went and wasted the whole thing on drugs. Very fast. Within about three months, nothing was left. I asked him, 'Yotam, sweetheart, what's with the film, have you shot something yet?' The guy is very talented, I believed him. I wanted to do something nice with my money. But he put the whole thing into his veins and up his nose. And even now, that arrogant kid is still trying to bring me down."

I wanted to get up and go, wash off all that moisture, but I hadn't yet finished my business here.

"Come." Nukhi Azariya got up off the wet floor, and walked

with manly steps to the door of the sauna. There it was dark and too hot, as if we had gone from the paradise of kebabs and watermelon to hell. I went in behind him and he closed the door. We sat on a wooden bench and my pulse was racing.

"You don't feel good here?" he asked.

"It's too hot for the Land of Israel," I said. "Maybe it's good for Scandinavia."

"It's good, believe me, you've got to clean out everything from inside," and suddenly I thought that the person who should be here with him was Haim, because the two of them were big on issues of internal cleanliness.

"Listen, Nukhi," I said and moved a little closer to him; might as well go for it, hairy thigh next to hairy thigh. "I'm dealing with a very sensitive issue, impossible to go into detail now, but I'm asking you to let Yotam back into the city. That jerk doesn't interest me, I think of him exactly as you do. He's a total waste. But it has to do with the lives of other people. You must understand that . . . "

Now it was really hard for me to breathe . . .

Nukhi put his hand on me and asked: "Is it important for security?"

"Yes, Nukhi," I coughed. My breathing dried up as if we were on Mars. "It's very important for security. I wouldn't have come to bother you with nonsense."

His totem face remained opaque, he sat with slack limbs in his corner, poured water on his head, which brought up a mask of steam, until he said: "Someday I'll also need help. You'll come help me when I do? You won't forget me?"

I promised him on my word of honor, on my children I swore to him.

After we showered, we ate sorbet at a little table the pleasant Turkish woman set up for us. I felt a lot better than when I entered.

We drank coffee and Nukhi Azariya told me he was expanding his business: now he was dealing a lot in real estate investments abroad, mainly in Romania and Moldova, he knew important people there who were seeking security advice. "If you decide to resign and make a lot of money, come to me," he said. What can I say? The attentions of that piece of shit flattered me. "Of course I'll remember this," I muttered. I was fond of him. The man was resourceful and had a natural intelligence. You could do business with him.

Nukhi stayed there to continue his day of treatments, and I was tossed out to the vistas of the market. In the west, the sun was dying out in the purple sea behind some paddleball players. He's right, I said to myself; got to rest, eat better, enjoy screwing, soon it's over.

The house was empty now. Four rooms of solitude. I went into the child's room, sat on the little bed. He took the cars and Spiderman and all the rest with him. I longed to hear his voice. I turned the CD player on; inside was a disk of lullabies that Sigi had sung to him at bedtime. He's a good child, I thought, a curious and smart child. I didn't talk with him and didn't listen to him and didn't devote any attention to him. I miss you, Papa, I want you to come home on time, I miss you, he'd say childishly on the phone, and I didn't understand that somebody could really love me like that. Until he stopped.

What could I do alone in an empty house, except drink the rest of a bottle of whiskey I once bought from the duty free shop, a liquid that remained forever like every good poison, take a book from the shelf and put it back, I could no longer believe the stories somebody makes up, turn on the television and burn out my brain in front of it, eat with my hands from the refrigerator, shower until my skin turned red, look at myself in the mirror—I never was handsome—look for pictures in an album, close it in sorrow, drink some more? I almost went to the interrogation installation to volunteer for night duty. And they won't let me do that now, either.

The *etrog* man suddenly talked to me. He lived in a room he rented from some Greek locals in a village in the mountains. They had strange rites that fascinated him. They made statues and painted murals. The ground was fertile and life was calm. The air was clean of the nervousness and bitterness of the Jews. He waited in the village until the *etrogs* were almost ripe. Below, in the harbor, the ship waited to take him back with the cargo to the Land of Israel. He thought of sending it on its way, cutting off his return route. Everything there looked like the Garden of Eden: the groves, the sky, the springs, the clean people who wore scarlet shirts. In the Land of Israel, there was desolation and destruction, as if an atomic bomb had fallen . . . My eyes shut from the whiskey in the middle of writing. I wanted to bring Daphna some new pages that were nicely written, but the letters blurred. I thought of my child and the other children we didn't have. The people on the shore of Gaza, not far from here, have ten or twelve children and support them on nothing, on a little white flour for pitas, give birth to so many of them and without fear despite the shortage. A father of ten children sits across from me, who am I to interrogate him at all? He's got a whole tribe to educate and feed and house. Other faces passed before my mind's eye, scared and grimacing with pain and sneering and laughing contemptuously and dead. Take the handcuffs off them, sit across from them, release the guards behind the door, endanger yourself, be a man, stop this nightmare . . .

I lay down in bed. I found a quiet tune on the radio. Instead of calming, the whiskey made me aggressive and restless. My heart was pounding. I got up and checked the medicine cabinet to see if Sigi had left something behind, sometimes she takes a little pill, but everything was empty as after a search. I could go for a run now, kill myself on the road, calm the raging body, if I weren't lying poured out and drunk on the bed.

Shortly before midnight, I called Daphna. I tried not to sound drunk. I told her that Yotam could come back to the city,

I talked with the man, he promised not to hurt him. "What are you doing up at this hour, Daphna?"

"You sound funny. Have you been drinking?"

"A little," I said. There was no reason to lie. "My wife and child went abroad. I'm left alone."

"I couldn't fall asleep either," she said. "I'm rereading Hani's stories. He's sleeping here on the sofa next to me."

"Yotam can come back," I brandished again the spoils I had brought her. "I talked with Nukhi Azariya. He won't touch him."

"I don't know what Yotam will do in the city," said Daphna. "He doesn't have any anchor here."

"That's what you wanted, isn't it?" I said in the dark.

"I know," she said. "You fulfill your obligations. You're obedient. That's fine."

We agreed I'd come the next day. I also picked up Hani's thin book. I turned on the reading lamp next to the bed. Fishermen come back from the sea with a few flounder in their net, the vegetable market, the sand in the alleys, bright-eyed children. Sad, little stories, almost without a plot, lacking energy. The book remained open on my chest when I fell asleep.

I came to her the next evening. The apartment looked like a field hospital. Yotam opened the door to me in his underwear, limping ridiculously; his leg had developed an infection caused by a dirty needle. His foggy eyes indicated that he had taken something. "Oh, aha, it's you," he neighed. "You came to collect the payment, come sit down, take a seat in the waiting room."

"Mother, an honored guest has arrived," he declared mockingly; what he said could barely be understood, and he tottered off to the inside rooms.

Hani was sitting upright in an armchair in the living room, well dressed, looking like an Egyptian mummy, as if he were afraid death would catch him in pajamas.

"Just a minute," Daphna called from the bathroom.

I stood in the doorway of the living room. A strip of plaster was peeling from the ceiling. Downstairs in the street, a crazy driver was honking. "Come sit down," Hani invited me and turned his head slowly. "Why are you standing in the doorway?"

I came to him and asked how he felt. His bag fell on the carpet and his hands were shaking as he tried to catch it and push it back into its hiding place.

"Pretty good," said Hani. "The medicines help. It barely hurts now."

"I read your stories," I said. "I liked them."

He was glad, his cheeks were sunk deep into their bones, and he made a dismissive gesture. "It's like pictures in the sand," he said. "They may be nice for a moment, then the sea washes them away. Thank you very much, *habibi*."

We sat in silence. Daphna lingered in the bathroom. That was the right moment to move ahead with him. I asked if he missed Gaza.

"What's to miss there," he laughed. "You don't miss a place like that. Maybe I miss people, not Gaza. It's hell. I miss my children, who aren't there anymore."

I asked how many children he had. I had to be empathic with him, devoid of all aggression, I tried very hard.

"Only two," he said. "A son and a daughter. The daughter got married a few years ago and moved to Kuwait."

"And the son?" I asked.

"The son," he sighed. "The son isn't here either."

Daphna came out washed and wearing makeup and a tight dress. Her shoulders were strong and gleaming.

"Come on, we're going out," she declared. "I'll just ask Yotam if he wants to come with us."

Dull syllables were heard from the inside rooms, he raised his voice in a shriek for a moment. Daphna came out less jolly than when she had gone in.

I asked where we were going. "To a party," she answered, and started down the stairs.

"Wait a minute." I ran after her. "I thought we had a lesson, I wrote some new pages . . . " But she galloped down. I won't say I didn't enjoy watching her.

Daphna sat between us in the back seat of the cab. She opened the window, even though it was damp and hot outside, because she didn't like the cold of the air-conditioner. The cab driver sat alone as we headed for the sea. The last of the swimmers was climbing onto the boardwalk, suburban families were ambling back and forth with strollers, from Charles Chlor Park rose pillars of smoke smelling of meat. I silently tallied the attacks that had occurred on that short stretch of beach; I stopped at four and wasn't sure I remembered them all; after every one of them I had been up all night. At that moment, with Daphna's orange blossom perfume in the air, they felt like a bad dream. At the Dolphinarium, the driver turned left, toward Neve Tzedek. Daphna was happy, getting out inspired her. "She's an awful writer," said Daphna. "But awful rich, and she's got a fantastic house. They bought it from the Shalosh family for more than two million dollars, God knows how much it's worth now. They publish her books only because of these parties. And she bribes her editor, everybody knows that."

The big house was surrounded by a high fence and a jasmine hedge. A guard delayed us at the entrance, Hani and I looked suspicious to him, but just before it got embarrassing, Daphna pulled us inside. Our hostess, the writer, stood in the gigantic entrance hall—the ceiling was twice as high as the one in our cottage in Ra'anana—and greeted the guests with kisses on their cheeks. We got ours, too. "How beautiful you look," the hostess said to Daphna. "You forever seem to be growing, all the time like a teenage boy." I liked that comparison. We followed Daphna's dress up the internal staircase to the crowded terrace. On one side were the lights of the seashore, and on the other side were the high towers of the financial center. Daphna quickly blended in, flooded with smiles; Hani and I were left leaning on the concrete ledge above the quiet street. I saw that it was hard for him to stand like that. I brought a lemonade for Hani and a beer for me, and I also got him a chair. We were swallowed up by the gigantic plants. Here and there, I recognized a famous face. A dwarf olive tree planted in a big ceramic pot loomed over us. There was a fine wind from the sea and German artisan beers, standard serving girls, with the interesting faces of acting students, who walked around with small elaborate snacks. Now and then, Daphna brought some victim to introduce to us. I tried my best to engage in small talk. Hani had more patience and talent for that, and so it turned out I was silent and he talked, generally about people and places he had known in his happy years in Tel Aviv. There were cultured people there, handsome women, the kind who liked to bad-mouth me and my companions, but that evening I was a literary novice, a lover of man, standing and slowly getting drunk enveloped in the free spirit circulating on that charming terrace above Neve Tzedek.

Hani turned into a kind of social highlight. Everyone was glad to meet an authentic Arab, and from Gaza to boot, as if a guest from the moon had landed among them. They were comfortable with Hani, who spoke good Hebrew and was pleasant and polite. When they brought up politics, he evaded the subject with a smile. Women touched him affectionately, he radiated happiness and plunged among them, glad of the attention. I stood on the side like an angry adolescent.

I saw that Hani was getting tired. I went to him and asked if he needed anything, maybe to go to the bathroom, or to take his medicine, and he said he was all right, he felt good here, there hadn't been such open air for a long time. "You're not angry at them?" I whispered to him.

"Why should I be angry?" he said. "They're good people. Are you angry at them?" he looked at me uncomprehending.

Fragments of conversation rose to me on the wind, the normal talk of people like them, who have no responsibility, who don't have to get their hands dirty. I saw one of my history professors. I tried to get close to him and hear what he was talking about, but he gave me an empty look; he had no idea who I was. I went back to the ledge, which had become my safe haven.

In the middle of the party on the roof, a newspaper photographer arrived with big lenses and a photographer's vest and started firing his flash in all directions. I turned back toward the sea so he wouldn't catch me, God forbid, and publish a picture of me with Hani; that could destroy the whole business. In general, I didn't want to be photographed, like Indian women who are afraid the camera will steal their soul. Daphna came and took me by the arm. "Come, let's walk around a little, meet people, you're so sullen." She got into a conversation with a young writer whose last book she admired; I had read some decent reviews of his work. He had horn-rimmed glasses and abundant hair. "Meet a friend," she said to him. "This is my mystery man," and she held me close to her. I had to squeeze out a smile. Her touch was nice and cool, my bare arm clung to her thin shoulders. Afterward, her friend came to us, an older woman. Daphna whispered to me that she was also very rich— after her husband left her, she got a wad of money, and now she lived most of the time with a young man in India. We circulated like that until we came to my history professor, who was now willing to relate. "He studied with you," Daphna revealed to him, and he smiled at me politely. Very slowly, I began feeling less strange, and the anger melted a little, the cocktails and the wine I drank helped, but above all it was thanks to the proximity of Daphna, who didn't move from my side. Now and then I'd have to push a camera lens away from my face so I wouldn't be photographed, until Daphna whispered, "Stop that."

"Let's go see what's with poor Hani," she said. We found him deep in conversation with the hostess, who recalled that she had met him once at a café on the Herbert Samuel Quay, many years ago. He had invited everybody at the table to come visit him in Gaza, promised he'd show them around and protect them from all harm. "Where did you disappear?" she asked Hani. "As if the earth had swallowed you." Hani laughed lightly and muttered something. I brought him a bowl of fruit, watermelon cut in cubes and a bunch of grapes, and the writer's husband who seemed to be an open and genial man joined us, and suddenly we had a group. It had been a long time since I had sat with normal people like that.

We returned in a cab laughing cheerfully, all of us a little drunk. Daphna again sat between the two of us. Only the jerk of a cabdriver gave Hani a sour glance now and then in the rearview mirror. I could have throttled him.

Daphna's street was deserted now, the lights in the windows were out, bats flapped their wings among the dark branches of the ficus trees. I felt bad about leaving them. Daphna supported Hani up the long flight of stairs.

Tomorrow I could report to Haim that I had made progress.

It turned out that the relatives of the fat young man who died sued the state for damages. I was called to an urgent meeting with the lawyer handling the case. She had a small office, filled with files coming out of every hole, all the cabinets were bursting with paperwork. When I entered, she was finishing a stormy call, there was some problem with a nanny who didn't come. I waited patiently in the door and asked whether I should come back some other time. "No, come in. I've got to present the defense brief the day after tomorrow and I don't have any idea what to write."

I sat down across from her—behind her was the high tower of the defense ministry, full of dishes and relays dripping radiation into the brains of those sitting in the offices—and waited for questions.

Very slowly and methodically, she went through that night

with me step-by-step, didn't leave out a minute, insisted on not skipping over a moment. She wanted me to draw the room for her, where he was sitting and where I was. How he was tied. Did we beat him. "Show me exactly how he was tied up," she asked. I didn't see any empathy in her eyes.

"I'd need a much lower chair," I told her up close. "And handcuffs."

She asked if the doctor had seen him before the interrogation. "I don't think so," I said. "We don't check whether they're able-bodied." The lawyer didn't laugh. She was a good-looking woman, with swarthy skin and big eyes and she didn't smile once. "Explain to me how he died," she asked finally.

I really didn't want to go back to that, to the choking, the death rattles, the look of imminent disaster on his face when he knew he wasn't getting out of it. She insisted I tell her everything. I had a fit of pesky, dry coughing, and she got up to bring me a glass of water. She had long legs in tailored trousers.

When she came back I asked if she was for me or against me because, so far, I hadn't understood from her questions. "It's not a personal case," she said. "I'm defending the state, so it won't have to pay too much money. From what I've heard so far, that won't be simple."

"You really don't understand what happened there?" I tried to explain more forcefully. "Recall that a ticking bomb was walking around, we had to catch him."

She insisted on continuing with a precise description of the details—what we did after he lost consciousness, how long until the medic arrived—until I was fed up, her small office and the papers were suffocating me, and so was the accusation in her eyes. I asked again, quietly, if it wouldn't be enough for her to write to the judge that it was all done to save lives, to prevent murder.

"What does that have to do with it?" she asked. She also seemed fed up. "Is that a reason to choke him?"

I banged on the table and said in a loud voice, almost shouting: "Nobody choked him, the man was sick, he choked by himself."

"That's not what the interrogator with you said. He said you put your hands on his throat."

By now I no longer remembered exactly what had happened there. The foam bubbling from the mouth, the desperate look, the picture of the children we found in his pocket. I sat silent, I didn't have the strength to defend myself anymore. What did he tell you, that young dog?

"I read your internal report," she went on whipping. "That your emotional state was not optimal at that time. Can you detail that issue for me? What were you going through?"

"That's none of your business," I said. "I was in excellent shape. I entered the interrogation room humming tunes from the army choirs. Twelve years I've worked in this, and no day is a holiday, believe me. I was friendly and warm and empathic. Calm and tranquil. Loving and hugging. Choking and abusing. You sent me there, madam, why are you complaining about me?"

"I sent you?" she laughed, perplexed. "I don't even know you."

"What do you intend to do with what they told you? With the choking and the binding and the killing in that cell? Do you intend to take it outside, stop the horror? Come on, do something. You're a woman of the law. Take it into your own hands."

That shut her up. She looked at me like I was a lunatic. I knew she'd give a full report on our meeting, but I didn't care anymore. I was finally fed up with all that stinking hypocrisy.

"You don't care," I went on assailing her. Outside there was a gray sunset and the office was lit by a florescent lamp. "Because you'll never go there. And nobody you know will ever go there, not even to visit. You don't want to hear anything. Let them be locked up tight in cages, those human apes, so they can't escape, let their mouths be gagged with rags so they won't shout. All that . . . "—A framed family picture at the edge of the desk caught my attention, a handsome Israeli man, perpetual student by the look of it, good! two children wearing ski clothes, someplace foreign—"All that so they won't come devour your great legs and your children and your sweet husband."

Suddenly a small tic appeared at the corner of her mouth, oops, another one; I was happy I had shaken her arrogant serenity. "The whole thing is so shocking," she mumbled to herself. Then her tone changed and in an official voice she said she would call me to testify when the time came.

I had a desire to take her hand, that good woman, go down in the elevator with her and walk with her on the sidewalk until we came to that place in the photo, until the two of us were released.

Four or five people crowded around the table in Haim's office. We were joined by a few external agents who were cooperating with us on the project. I briefed them on my progress with Hani, trying to impress them with my seriousness. I spoke concretely, I didn't embarrass anyone.

The partners said they were interested in carrying out the action within ten days, for all kinds of reasons; afterward it might be too late. Our conversation was manly and practical. Afterward, I went to meet Daphna. She asked to see me urgently. I didn't want to meet in a café again; the last experience was enough for me, I had felt as if I were in a display window. So she suggested we meet at the university pool.

The summer vacation was over and the pool was almost empty. A few devoted swimmers with time on their hands swam back and forth until they had done their daily number of lengths. I was sorry I had stopped swimming. After fifty laps, the head is cleansed of all foolishness. I spotted an orange bathing cap in the water and a long body that looked like her.

The body I attributed to her was swimming well, skimming over the water with long movements, breathing with every third movement. She had a professional approach. She wore the full black bathing suit, cut high at the thigh and with a white stripe.

I sat under an umbrella, bought something to drink, focused on the small hovering shadow that accompanied her on the bottom. The sun scorched the lawns mercilessly. I counted the movements she made from one end to the other, forty-six, forty-seven, without any effort at all, she seemed to be able to swim forever. Finally, she stood in the transparent water, took off her swim goggles and the cap, shook her hair from side to side, like a dog, rested in the water another moment, and climbed up the ladder. God, what legs she had.

She rinsed herself under the shower at the entrance to the pool, dried herself, slipped her feet into flip-flops, put on sunglasses. I waved to her from afar, and she came to me.

"Hi," she said, and sat down in the chaise longue across from me. "Can you get me something to drink?"

At the counter, I ordered fresh orange juice for the two of us. She crossed her legs and said: "So nice when you finish . . . "

I said that she swam very nicely, that I was very impressed. "Thanks," she laughed. Up close you could see, a few fine wrinkles on her face. "I trained with the 'Future Maccabees' youth team. That's where the improved style comes from."

Her laugh was clear. Not far from us, a crow cawed nonstop, as if he had lost his nestling.

Daphna sipped the juice and then stretched out her legs and leaned her head on the back of the chair, as if she had fallen asleep. She had the movements of a glamour girl. I thought of how she had looked twenty years ago and what the hell she had done with all those jerks. There was a red blossoming on the trees and a distant sprinkler began spinning on the lawn, and heat mists rose around us. Now the two of us were the only ones in the whole area.

"Jump into the water a little," she said. "Cool down. You look upset. Did you hear anything from the wife and child?"

I muttered something, and she didn't press. Her feet were close to me now, and I had a desire to grab them and see her response.

The lifeguard, an elderly man with a broad-brimmed hat, passed us and asked how we were and she answered with the warmth of an old friend. She didn't look as if anything was really at stake. Why was it so urgent to bring me here?

"You were great at that party," she said. "Hani also enjoyed it. He thinks good things about you. He asked what you do for a living. I told him you had made a lot of money in the stock market. He was very impressed by that. He said you remind him a little of his son. You don't intend to kill him, right?"

"Who?" I jumped. Slivers of sun burst in my brain.

"Anybody. You won't kill anybody," she said, and the picture split into snapshots, as on a broken computer screen.

"Why did you call me?" I asked.

"I need money," said Daphna. "Hani is costing me a lot, and the kid is also living with me now. The bank won't give me a loan. You think you could help me with that?"

Now I was in familiar territory, my natural milieu. And yet I felt nauseated, for some reason I hoped it would remain pure with her.

"How much do you need?" I asked. She named a sum, relatively high for what we pay those in the field, who are willing to sell their mother for a thousand shekels.

"I'll have to get permission for that," I said. "It's a lot of money."

"Tell them I'm a high-priced call girl," she laughed—suddenly she had orange tints in her hair—"and you're a pretty high pimp, and somebody needs to finance the whole operation. Otherwise we'll split up, me and you. The *etrog* man will have to look for another teacher. Even though it's fun to sit on the lawn with you. You don't talk much. Were you always so taciturn?"

I felt scorched, as if she had breathed fire on me. I used to come to meetings with Arabs with money in my pocket, petty cash, a few bills would settle the issue. She was talking about a salary. "Over the years, it developed," I answered. "I prefer to listen. I don't have a lot to say."

Daphna got up and said she had to go take a real shower before the chlorine ate her skin and hair. I watched her strong body from behind as she strode toward the dressing rooms. When does the collapse come for a woman like that? The crow didn't stop screaming. The water in the pool glowed blue. I tried to imagine the touch of our bodies in the great heat.

Afterward, Haim authorized the sum she asked for over the phone, but told me to haggle with her a little; she shouldn't think she could get whatever she wanted. "Move fast now," he said in his most serious voice. "This is a house of cards. I don't want everything to depend on that whole circus you've been building around you. Too many clowns and acrobats. Our job is to deliver the goods, others will do the rest. Start tying up the package."

Tying it up good, that was the whole thing. Tying it up good and bringing in the fastened package. Afterward, throw it away. The rest isn't our business.

Sigi called from Boston on Saturday night, woke me up from a sound sleep, demanded I talk with the child on Skype.

"I don't know how to use that," I grumbled. "Why don't we talk on the phone."

"He wants to see you," she explained. "Go to the computer, it's all set up there, make an effort for the child."

I did as she said. The picture was blurry and the voice sounded metallic. Sigi sat him at the camera as in a kidnappers' video. From his chatter, I gathered that he was going to kindergarten, that he already had two friends, a high slide, squirrels were climbing a tree. Mother bought him a car in a big store and afterward they ate pizza without any cheese at all. He talked continuously and I didn't interrupt him.

"When are you coming, Papa?" he asked.

"Soon, when I finish working," I answered.

He went on with his childish talk. I tried to gather my child from the piecemeal, interrupted fragments of the picture.

"Is Mother there?" I asked, and he turned from the camera and called her. The picture of him changed into a wall, until Sigi came on. The familiar frame of her face, something with her hair had changed, maybe the curls were cut short.

"I'm turning off the camera if you don't mind," she said, and I was left with just the voice.

"Why, Sigi . . . ," I said.

I got a technical report in a few sentences: work was excellent, she was very happy she had come, the child was adjusting well to the kindergarten. She didn't say my name even once.

"I want us to separate," she said suddenly. The sound was as clear as could be asked from an instrument, everything is science in discussions now. "We've got to cut it off. It's not healthy for anyone, especially not the child."

"Wait," I said, choked up. "I . . . "

I wanted her to put herself back up on the screen; face to face, it's easier to persuade. I wanted her to call me by name at least once, I even chuckled strangely. Sigi's head was completely artificial.

"You sound troubled," she said. "It's lucky it has nothing to do with me now."

"I'll come to you and we'll talk," I threw out in desperation. "Maybe I'll get a job in the consulate, I'll be a guard or something, I'll identify Middle Eastern guys walking around at the entrance."

"I don't want you to come," Sigi decreed through the ads

popping up on the screen. "I'm not waiting for you anymore. There's nothing between us anymore."

I asked her to call the child back. My heart went out to him. I knew he was hiding around the corner, listening to every word, feeling everything and understanding everything.

"He's playing and I don't want to disturb him," said Sigi. The line went dead.

Daphna, Hani and I were sitting above the sea in Margaret Thayer's restaurant in Jaffa, eating lunch on the tab of the general security services.

Hani wanted to come here, he remembered the place from long ago, when Victor Thayer was still alive and broadcast election ads. He remembered the couscous and the fish.

Hani was thin as a skeleton, you couldn't mistake his disease. He touched only crumbs of the food. But he was smiling, looking far out to sea, a delicate and nice man. Daphna offered him some of her food, put it in his mouth. "Very good, excellent," he said and relented.

Margaret came out of the kitchen to greet us, shaking her wet hands. For a moment I worried that she'd recognize me from somewhere. She examined me for a moment from afar, and then took a chair and sat down next to Daphna and they started fishing up forgotten things.

"How is your kid?" asked Margaret. "You used to bring him when he was a baby, even at night. Everybody said how beautiful he was. The whole group used to play with him."

"He's fine, finding himself," answered Daphna and her eyes gave away the lie to the whole world. "Hani missed your food," said Daphna.

"Of course I remember you," said the owner. "You'd talk with Victor about fish. What happened to you, where did you disappear?"

Hani answered her with a sad smile. Margaret went back to

the kitchen. Meanwhile, a few tables around us had filled up. Daphna ordered a bottle of cold white wine.

"I'll drink," sighed Hani. "In Gaza they would have killed me. Not so bad, just one little glass. God will forgive me for that."

The air was still, and the sea stood in a tub that ended at the gray line of the city. Daphna said she was sorry she'd never gone to visit him there; there was always a fear they'd toss grenades, stab, but now it's worse.

"It's very close," Hani sipped a few drops from his glass. "The same sea. Exactly the same sun. Only with a lot of fences in the middle."

"Someday all the fences will fall, we'll all be together," said Daphna. The sea and the wine colored her eyes turquoise.

"That will happen after us, *habibati*," laughed Hani and gently put his sick hand on hers. "Today the lunatics decide what to do. The sea doesn't interest them. They miss the mountains."

I finished the bottle slowly and quietly, and crunched the heads of mullets between my teeth.

"Only a cigarette is missing," said Hani. "How good it would be to smoke once."

"What about your children?" Daphna suddenly asked him. "Don't you want to see them?"

I almost choked on a bone. I bit my lips. My eyes stared at the rickety tourist boat that never had any tourists.

"Want to," said Hani. "But the daughter has four children and she can't leave them. And the son . . . ," he laughed. "That kid can't come in here. He's not as nice as his father. He was a prisoner, you know, they kept him in prison camp in the desert for three years, and now . . . "

"Where is he now?" asked Daphna, as if she wanted to reward me for the meal.

"God knows," Hani smiled in embarrassment, and looked

into my eyes, seeking understanding in them. "Knocking around the world."

We ate *malabi,* a kind of flan, and drank mint tea for desert, that really was a splendid meal. Daphna wanted to pay the bill, made a whole production; I took out a card and she pulled out cash and in the end, I let her pay.

On the way to the car, we leaned on the ledge, looked at the rock of Andromeda. Hani said his father missed that corner of the world, for him it was the most beautiful place on the whole planet. We sat Hani in the back seat, he was tired, and Daphna sat next to me. "You want to make a tour, Hani?" she asked him. "See a little of Jaffa?" And he said he'd be glad, only if I wasn't in a hurry.

"It's fine," I said. "I'm not in a hurry. The stock market went very well this morning, I've already made my daily tab."

We drove along the road leading to the port. Now the sea rose a little and waves crashed on the wall. We passed a new white mosque built there, Al-Bahar Mosque, the mosque of the sea, what a nice name. I went back to the square of the clock. "See how they've renovated the clock," said Daphna and Hani laughed: "The sultan must be very happy."

After Halbani's hummus stand, I turned right into Agmi—a lot of scaffolding, renovations, new cars, Jews coming to live in the old houses—and I drove along the sea to the border of Bat Yam.

"Where is your house?" asked Daphna.

"We'd already moved," said Hani. "If I'm not mixed up. I didn't live here. It's all from stories. I was a baby after all."

"Are you angry?" asked Daphna.

"I'm sad," said Hani. And after some thought, he added: "That I should have to miss a place I never knew."

We drove back to Tel Aviv through the flea market. The celebration of lunch vanished in the rush hour traffic jam. I set the radio on some medieval music, Daphna said that felt good. I helped Hani up the stairs, three flights, in fact I dragged him on my shoulder. "You're a good man," he said to me when we got there. "I like you."

In the apartment, a smell of burning came from the inside rooms. Daphna stood frozen in the doorway.

"Go to him," she asked me. "I simply can't."

I went down the short corridor and opened the door without knocking. Yotam was sitting erect with a syringe stuck in his arm, a cord blocking veins, and an expression of definite pleasure on his face. Got to try it once, I thought. I closed the door quietly and went back to the entrance.

Daphna looked at me with tears in her eyes. "Don't go in there," I said.

"I can't bear it," she wept and clutched my hand. "What should I do, tell me, what to do?"

"In the end, we'll take care of him, soon, soon, after it's all over," I whispered to her, and she slowly let go, leaving red marks on my hand.

Hani was in the armchair where I had put him. "I'll go talk to the kid," said the Arab man. His voice rose sudden and firm.

"No, don't go," shouted Daphna and looked at me. "He can kill you."

I wanted to get away. It had become too crowded in that crumbling apartment. But I forced myself to take one more step. "Maybe we'll get together tomorrow," I said, bending over Hani. "Let's go to the movies."

"Yes, why not," the eyes of my new dying friend lit up.

The next day, Hani was waiting for me right on time. Avital Ignats's old clothes were hanging on him as on a hanger, the best men's fashions of the seventies. Daphna helped him down the stairs and I dragged down the folding wheelchair.

The chair was pretty rickety and one wheel squeaked. I pushed him slowly down the slope of Frishman Street, like a welfare aid worker from Albania who missed home. Hani felt like talking, more and more. He told how much he loved Tel Aviv: he'd had a good time here, a lot of friends, staying out till the middle of the night, interesting conversations, went to a lot of plays, performances. Asked if Dani Litani was still performing, he was his friend; he also remembered Zahuira Harpai, a wonderful and very funny woman. "Back then I started writing a story about Jaffa," said Hani, "but I couldn't finish it."

"Where did you live?" I asked, trying to get the broken wheel out of a crack in the sidewalk.

"Mainly with Daphna," answered Hani, seated in the rickety chair as in a royal chariot. "Until Ignats would come. Ignats didn't like me being in his house. He was a very nervous man. Smoked a lot. Drank a lot. Couldn't make the movies he wanted, and took it all out on her. He didn't know how to treat her nice."

We passed the large excavation on Frishman at the corner of Dizengoff. A big poster showed a drawing of the skyscraper that would be built there, luxury apartments for culture merchants. "You're always building," he said. "Towers to the sky. Look what you've got and what we've got, the same land, the same ground, the same sand. You've got everything and we've got nothing. But you're nervous. You don't have the patience we do."

Across the street, some woman I knew passed by, I didn't remember exactly where I knew her, maybe from the army, maybe from Sigi's work. She lingered a moment to look at me, looked to be in two minds about crossing the street to say hello, but went on. I felt embarrassed.

"I thank you very much," said Hani, apparently sensing something. "Too bad we didn't know each other when I was healthy."

"Why did you leave Tel Aviv?" I asked innocently.

"Oh, that was some story," said Hani. His head moved from side to side under me. "Somebody denounced me. They took me for interrogation, I sat in jail a few days, they didn't treat me very nice. In the end they let me out on condition that I wouldn't go back in, that I wouldn't come visit you anymore."

"Were you arrested?" I asked. "Why did they do such a thing to you?"

"Oh, nothing serious really, they gave me a few smacks, they didn't let me sleep . . . Really, I'm sorry I'm telling you that."

"That's awful," I said. "Why did they do that to you? Why did they act like that with such a nice man as you?" I almost blurted out an hysterical laugh at my silly questions.

"I wasn't connected to anything, but they thought I was a terrorist. After they understood I wasn't a terrorist, they wanted me to spy for them in Gaza. Maybe I'm agreeable, love Jews, but I'm not a traitor. They told me I wouldn't get out, they'd give me ten years for knowing members of the PLO. I was with them for five days, I came out five years older."

"How come you don't hate us?" I asked. My shirt was covered with spots of sweat from going up the concrete ramp of the square and the hard work of pretending.

"Why should I hate?" laughed Hani and turned his face up to me. "I'm a weak man, I can't hate. Maybe I'm not a man. Can't take revenge, that's how I am. There are wicked people among you, but for Daphna, I'd give my life."

Up in the square, the fountain was revolving and the music player wasn't working. We went down the other side. A damp orange light poured over the city through the spaces between the buildings. A group of girls in shorts came toward us, giggling, and Hani smiled at them. The guard in the door of the center checked us casually, he didn't check the wheelchair at all, you could bring twenty pounds of explosives in it loaded with nails and whatever you want.

I parked the chair before the movie posters. I hadn't been to the movies in years, maybe since the child was born. Hani hadn't seen anything either since the golden years of the American cinema in the seventies, so the two of us wanted to choose carefully. We argued a little: he wanted to go to a romantic French film and I explained to him that he was making a bad mistake, they always fail with their films. In the end, the two of us decided on a film that won the last Oscar.

I bought a big box of popcorn and two Cokes. We ate from the same box. I moved him slowly from the wheelchair to a seat on the aisle. The air conditioning was excellent. When the light went out, I gave a sigh of relief—what a joy, now I could shut up and cut myself off from the world—and I saw that he was also smiling with joy like a child. Five in the evening, the whole world is running around, going nuts, and we, at long last, are sitting in the movies.

We weren't disappointed. The movie really was good. The two of us fell in love with the star, Jennifer Connolly; the story was convincing, we sank into it for two hours and were sorry when it ended. "No more movie?" laughed Hani when the titles came up at the end. On the way out, I saw him looking longingly at MacDonald's; I understood that he must never have eaten their crap. I ordered him a Big Mac; he left almost the whole thing on the plate, but said politely that he liked it a lot. We talked about the film. Hani said the one thing he regretted in his life was that he wasn't born in Hollywood and hadn't made films like those.

"Nobody's born in Hollywood," I said. "You get there."

"But nobody from Gaza gets there," he laughed.

Hani said he'd try to walk, the film made him feel better, but after a few steps, he collapsed into my arms. I wheeled him back along Dizengoff. We passed the place where the Number 5 bus blew up across from the shwarma stand—I got there back then along with the body collectors—I almost blurted out something because we were so close, but I kept quiet. The street was full of sooty traffic, an Eastern trance accompanied us for a moment from a passing sports car. Sadness and self-pity grabbed me, and almost made me cry. A bad smell rose from him, apparently his bag had filled up.

He asked if I had a wife. I told him I had a wife and child, and she had gone to work in Boston. He said in that case both of us were alone. Only I'm still alive, *habibi*, and walking on my own two feet, and you're very close to going down, I said to myself.

Now I was getting hungry and I suggested we sit down in a café and have something to eat. Why not, he said politely, I'd be very happy to do that. We sat down in an Italian-style café on the corner of Gordon Street. I maneuvered his chair to the bathroom and through the door and made sure he'd manage with all his arrangements.

"Everything's shit," he laughed when he came out of there and sat down in the chair. Suddenly he had the face of a bastard Arab, like the ones I could shake down for some small secrets about friends and relatives.

The waitress had beautiful skin and her face was beaming. The two of us noticed and looked at her the same way, with an admiration that will go down into the grave with us. I ordered a Milano style sausage sandwich, and to my surprise, Hani asked for pasta. As if he had decided to reward himself on our outing for all the years of hunger in Gaza. I finished my beer before the food came and ordered another one.

Hani told about the friends he had in Tel Aviv, mentioned names of cafés that had closed and books that were forgotten and people who had faded to nothing or had died; he talked about Daphna, who, whenever and wherever she appeared, was like a princess. "We're weak and ugly humans," he said. "But she's like the ocean, a force of nature, she's a diamond."

I took a picture of the child out of my wallet, not a recent picture, and put it on the table next to him. Hani looked at it up close and said he looked like me, but you can see he has a beautiful mother. He dropped food on the picture and the sauce stained it. He was very apologetic and tried weakly to wipe it off with the napkin. The child was entirely covered with oily sauce. I took the picture and buried it back in my wallet.

Hani looked very tired. I asked if he wanted to go home. His plate was still full. "You must miss your child," said Hani. I had to bend over to him to hear. "I remember my child when he was like that. The whole world I would have given for him. Afterward, you can't protect him. The world is stronger than you are, the world is bad . . . " Now he had tears in his eyes.

"How long has it been since you've seen your kid?" I asked. My muscles were tense, I hated the feeling of pressure before the crushing question, like a gorilla before the battle of his life. I wanted to go on talking with him man to man, without striving for any purpose.

"Almost six years," Hani replied. "Ever since he got out of jail." He told me the son had been imprisoned in a prison camp in the desert for two years, and after he got out, he left the country, couldn't find anything to do with himself in Gaza.

"Where is he now?" I asked.

In a person's look there is a blend of all kinds of things, and in Hani's look there was now also a percentage of suspicion. But only a little. I got beyond that barrier safely.

"Wandering around," said Hani, and sharply pushed away the plate of food. "God knows where he is now."

I knew exactly where he was. Haim had briefed me that very morning. The man had returned from Iran to Syria.

"And your daughter?" I asked, to allay suspicion.

"The daughter is in her house. She's got a good husband and good children."

"Because I thought . . . ," I began. "Listen, I've got quite a lot of money. I did very well in business in recent years. I can help you get together with your children. If they can't come here, maybe we'll arrange something outside. We can travel to a nearby place, Cyprus for instance. It shouldn't cost too much. You'll see the children for the last time. Think about that, Hani. I'd be glad to help."

Hani's response was strange. He started crying, simply bitter weeping. I had to get up to calm him down, stroke his gray hair. The beaming waitress came and asked if she could do something to help, maybe we wanted coffee and dessert.

Hani calmed down. There was silence between us. I was afraid I had exposed myself, that I was too coarse. An enormous moon rose in the distance, above the Azrieli Towers. Only when we got to her house, which was dark and stood like a ghost building among the renovated houses, did he say beneath me, from the squeaking wheelchair: "I want to go. I want to see the children. I hope you can arrange that."

Don't believe! I shouted inside myself. Refuse! But at the same time, the enormous joy of the hunter closing in on his prey exploded within me.

When I got upstairs with him, I was out of breath. Daphna was on the phone, feverish, gnawing her fingernails. She managed to tell me that Yotam had disappeared from the house two days ago and she had no idea where he was.

"Call me," I signaled to her after I had dragged Hani to his sofa, where he lay helplessly. On the round table in the kitchen was a big stack of pages, written in an intelligent hand; I picked up a few bright sentences, she was progressing nicely with her book. For a moment, Daphna came very close to me. Her eyes were somewhere else. My hands almost moved to embrace her waist. She moved away quickly and continued talking on the phone. What do you think you're doing! Don't you dare!

I stopped at the big supermarket on the way to Ra'anana, stood in the express line with my bedtime supplies: a bottle of Arak and a chocolate bar, almonds and red grapes.

Hani's son had been moving around the world for a few years now unknown to us. We hadn't noticed him until people started talking about him with respect. They relied on him. They gave him big sums of money. He came to Hezbollah head-quarters in Beirut. Moved to Damascus. Then he was sent to Iran to organize courses, arrange shipments of weapons, meet with senior operatives in the revolutionary guard. He was thirty-two years old, a serious man, a methodical worker.

He moved around freely. I was stuck between Ra'anana and Ashkelon and he was traveling in Sudan, Yemen, Djibouti, to all corners of the aristocratic Arab world, to all the places our clients went to get instructions, raise money, train. Even though he was cautious, things started coming together. He worked on several projects simultaneously, some of them routine, that con-cluded with a suicide bomber wraking havoc on Jewish flesh, and also on some big project whose details we couldn't figure out, causing us special concern. He put together the equipment, gathered the technicians, carefully chose the operatives; all our special means were useless. We still didn't know what it was.

The operation wasn't ours; the chance to help fell in our lap. Our job was to get him out of the dark holes to an exposed place where others could operate. He won't swallow that, he's too cau-tious, said Haim, he'd be very skeptical from the start. He'll never go to a non-Arab country. They've learned the lessons of previous liquidations.

I went with Haim to our neighbors on the hill to report on what was happening. There was always an aroma of the duty free shop about them, European clothes, an atmosphere of high tech. Haim and I came to them like a couple of venetian blind installers, one religious, plump, and limping, the other gray and taciturn. Ever since the project had begun, we had met with them for a weekly briefing. The previous meetings were drowsy, skeptical; this time there was some tension, the smell of prey was in the air.

The partners reported that his project was progressing: new equipment had arrived, the guy was visiting the training camps, they had all kinds of setbacks but they would apparently overcome them. The problem was we didn't know what they were planning.

"What will it achieve if we bring him down?" asked Haim, who loved to engage them in Talmudic dispute. "Their operation will go on even without him."

"He's the head," explained their representative, a fresh, ruddy guy who wore a light open-necked silk shirt. "He's the only one who knows all the details, everything is arranged in his head, all the connections are in his hands, without him, it won't work."

"Why not bomb the development site and destroy the operation?" asked Haim.

"Because we don't know where the operation is based," chuckled the partner. "We've only got hints, talk, movements. Nothing on the ground. We don't have an idea where it will go. There are too many possibilities. Could be anywhere in the world, from Thailand to America."

"So why will he come out of his hole now?" I asked. I didn't talk much during the meetings and my voice came out hoarse, precisely because I wanted to make an impression so they'd take me seriously.

"Because he loves his father an awful lot," smiled the redhead, who was tanned and fragrant as a yachtsman. "They've got great conversations between father and son on file, I wish my father and I had such relations. He misses him. He wants to say goodbye to him before he dies."

I was angry that they had milked Daphna's phone like a fat udder and didn't let me read the material. They shouldn't forget that it was I who brought him there. I'm the brains behind the whole thing.

"They mentioned you, by the way," said the man. "The

father said he knew a great guy, that if all the Jews were like him, the whole thing would be different. That you're a good Jew."

The table moved with a wave of laughter. I felt as if they had stood me on it naked with a dunce cap.

"What else do they talk about?" I asked quietly.

"Personal things," said the yachtsman tranquilly and leaned back. "About the father's health, the sister in Kuwait and her terrific children. The father brings up memories of Gaza, the seashore, how the two of them went fishing together. Yesterday, the son said he bought a rug in the market in Tehran and sent it to his sister. A few days ago, he described to his father the pyramids he saw in the desert of Sudan, he spoke about the ancient black kings who built them. It really made me want to go on a tour there in a jeep. Ask people who met him, they describe an intelligent, charismatic fellow, sharp as a razor. A monster has grown right before our eyes."

What else did Hani say about me? I thought. What did he say about Daphna? But around the table they moved to talk about flight instruments and means of dispatching, tiny submarines sold on the black market, all the nightmares that disturb their sleep.

"How much time do we still have?" asked Haim. Their meeting room was splendid, a big window open to the sea, insulated by three layers so no sound wave would leak out. I poured a bottle of bitter lemon into a glass of ice.

"No more than ten days," said the senior member, with cropped, graying hair, who, from the beginning of the meeting, had been looking at me skeptically and I didn't like it. "Just get him out for us to a place where we can work on him. You need anything? You lack anything?" he asked me patronizingly, the way I talk to the lowliest of my subordinates, those who keep me informed about what's on the menu in the Kasbah.

"We've got everything," Haim answered for me. "Just leave us alone for a few more days and we'll bring you the package."

"Just a few days," said their head and lit a cigarette. That amazed me—it had been a long time since I'd seen anybody smoke in a meeting, especially among those sterile characters. "We don't want the sky to fall on our head."

"Something about this story stinks, there are too many holes in the intelligence," said Haim on the way back.

"What do you want me to do?" I asked.

"Got to go on, no choice," said Haim. "We're only bit players, but right now the whole stage is yours. Everybody's looking at you. Everything depends on you. Everyday I report upstairs on what's happening. You've advanced very well with him. Just be careful now."

Haim got out of the car with great difficulty, hit the edge of the sidewalk and fell down, his *kippa* flew off his head. I quickly got out of the car to help him up. "I'm fine," he muttered when I grabbed him under the arms, as you hold a baby. "I'm not hurt, just my head is uneasy. Promise me that everything's fine. I don't want us to fail with this."

I called Daphna to invite myself for a lesson. I tried to sound relaxed so she wouldn't know how much I depended on her. "Hani's sleeping," she whispered. "We went to the doctor who raised his dosage across the board, otherwise he'd be going mad with pain. They don't give him more than a few weeks. The doctor said that was absolutely positively the end."

I went to town while waiting for Hani to wake up. I sat in a café, I looked at the girls, I bought a collection of Frank Sinatra records on sale, I walked from one end of Dizengoff Street to the other, past all the bridal shops. Evening had fallen and Daphna hadn't called, nor had she answered her cell phone. Just don't let him die on me, that nice Arab. But mainly I thought about her and what she was doing when she disappeared. I parked below the American embassy, at the sea. It was dark now. I sat in the car and my eyes closed to the sound of "Strangers in the Night."

In the middle of the night, the cell phone rang. The parking lot around me was empty, the windshield was foggy with night moisture. I raised the seat fast, shut up Frankie who was singing in an unending loop. "Come to Ikhilov," Daphna shouted. "They're slaughtering him, those whores."

I didn't know which of the two of them she was talking about, I didn't have time to ask, I raced with the blue siren into the damp screen of the night and went into the ambulance bay displaying the document that opens every door. I saw Daphna at the end of the emergency room, getting explanations from a young doctor in turquoise scrubs.

I went behind the curtain, recognized Yotam's thin white back as he lay naked on his belly.

The art of carving on the ass was very familiar to me from my work. Collaborators had their penis cut off and stuffed in their mouth, and on the other side, on the ass, they'd carve all kinds of drawings, depending on how talented the murderer was. After we caught them, they'd give all kinds of interesting explanations, sometimes about the myths of Islam and some-times about a basketball team.

They had given Yotam only an X on his behind, not too deep, but big. It took thirty colorful stitches to close him up. Daphna stood at his bed, her eyes swollen, trying to touch him, but he roared at her like an evil beast. From behind, you saw only long hair, an exposed back, a bandage. I went to the head of the bed to see his eyes. When he saw me, an awful smile of scorn and pain appeared on his face.

"What, my darling?" Daphna asked him, trying to stroke his head, offering him a glass of water. He answered her with a sti-fled roar. All around was the turmoil of a night in the emergency room, gurneys being moved back and forth, an incessant sound of distress hovered in the air. The doctor on duty left us and said somebody would soon come to take Yotam up to the ward.

The wounded boy mumbled something. Daphna wanted to

hear, she was so eager to get to him she almost fell. I heard him clearly from where I was standing. "Now the picture's perfect," he muttered with an effort. "Mother, man, and Yotam with an X on his ass. Your holy trinity is realized, Mother."

"Why do you talk to me like that?' she flinched, but came back to him immediately, touched his dirty hair. "It will pass," she told him. "They said they'd graft some skin and nothing will be seen."

"As far as I'm concerned, they can leave it," he squeaked. "I'll show my ass to people on Dizengoff and collect charity." He groaned with pain and Daphna went to look for the doctor to ask them to give him something for the pain.

"Morphine," he called after her. "Let them bring morphine."

"What happened?" I took the opportunity to go to him.

"Go," groaned Yotam. "Get out of here."

An orderly came and took him up to the ward. We waited in the corridor. People were passing by around us, staring at the gigantic bandage wrapping his loins, saw him lying twisted. It was a strange and despicable vision. "Why don't they get him into a room? Look how he's lying!" I said to the young doctor on duty who was sitting at the computer. "This isn't a private hospital here, sir," said the doctor. "At the moment, we've got a few more urgent cases. The guy is only scratched. He'll live."

Yotam was pleading non-stop for help. Daphna said some calming words to him, hugged him, tried to protect him from the evil looks all around.

"Give him more morphine, please," called Daphna. The doctor came to us in comfortable green German clogs, her ponytail jumped when she spoke. She said that Yotam had already gotten the maximum dose, any more was liable to kill him.

"He's a junkie," Daphna shouted. "The quantities you gave him don't move him. Please, go consult with someone. He's writhing in pain!"

"I'll find out," said the doctor. You could hear the contempt in her voice.

Daphna stood glued to the wall, shriveled. "How did that happen?" she asked with an accusing look. "You promised the area was clean. That he could come back. They found him tossed on the sidewalk in an alley behind Allenby Street, he couldn't stand up. My child was thrown into the gutter."

He was lucky they didn't take off his legs and leave half a body lying on the sidewalk, I thought, that also happens to people.

"I'll give him another dose," the doctor announced, emerging from the depths of the corridor. "I talked with my attending. He'll take responsibility for it and they'll clear a room for him right away. I'm sorry I was a little impatient before, I've got the shift from hell."

Daphna tried to smile with a face crushed with grief. "I'm sorry I burst out, you must not have slept since yesterday, and here I am yelling at you . . . "

The doctor stood facing her and then took her hand and they leaned on one another a moment. They laid Yotam at the end of a long room full of beds, at the window. The city was lighted beneath him. Daphna's eyes were lit with a red light and were flooded with tears.

Yotam got an IV with another dose of morphine and he began singing a song by Morrissey to himself. Daphna brought water and made him drink slowly, until the drugs kicked in and his eyes shut. That's what should be done with him, I thought, connect him to a sedative of drugs and let him sink. Take off.

I found two chairs and we sat at his bed. "I can't bear this anymore," whispered Daphna and put her head on me in the gloom, until her breathing became heavy and she sank into a sound sleep. I saw the lights of the houses go off and the streets empty and I heard groans of patients all around, but everything was fine: I could caress her head, protect it from all sides. In the hours remaining until morning, I was her only guard.

Haim called me on the cell phone in my shirt pocket as dawn broke and asked if I had seen the latest stuff. "No," I whispered, but Daphna had already woken up and was sitting up with her hair disheveled and barely remembered where she was until Yotam started pleading for more drugs. "Wait a minute," I told Haim and went out to the corridor.

"You're with her?" Haim asked suspiciously. "What are you doing together at such an hour?"

I told him all I could. He said that some bad stuff had come that made our issue very urgent. On high, they wanted us to make every effort to get the guy out immediately, they couldn't wait anymore.

I suggested to Daphna that she go wash her face, I'd take care of him in the meantime. I sat at Yotam's head and talked quietly into his ear, I asked questions. His sad twisted smile wasn't wiped off his face. Indeed, why are you interrogating him? I said to myself. What can he tell you? That he came to buy drugs and got mixed up with the street dealers? Maybe he owed them money, and they threw him on the stinking ground where there were once dunes and now only filth, told him that next week they'd be cutting in front, and then the throat.

When the doctors made their rounds, we were sent out of the room. We went down to drink coffee in the hospital cafeteria. I looked around and thanked my lucky stars that I wasn't yet dragging around a bag connected to my guts and didn't have an instrument stuck in my throat and was standing on my own two feet. "You promised me he could come back to town, that you guaranteed his safety," Daphna said again. You could measure her pulse by the contractions of anger in the blue vein in her neck.

"I thought you'd keep him at home," I justified myself. "I

can't protect him when he goes to buy drugs on the street. That doesn't even have anything to do with Nukhi Azariya."

Daphna fell silent. "That was bad from the start," she said gazing at nothing. "I sealed the kid's fate and he's not strong enough for it. I expected him to hold out. For years now, he hasn't called on me for help. And I look down on everything: I'm not like you, I'm not in your game, your prejudices don't touch me, my son was beautiful and strong and scared everyone; he's my sweet revenge. But he won't make it, that awful file is heavy on him and I don't help, I'm a coward . . . "

"Go rest, you're just hurting yourself," I said to her. "A kid can come out fucked even from the squarest family."

"No, I'll stay," said Daphna. "I have to make sure they take care of him. Anyway, I won't get any rest at home." A minute later, she shook herself. "Go to my house," she ordered me. "See what's with Hani. I left him alone like a dog. Give him something to eat and drink, see how he feels."

I stood under Daphna's house. The gorgeous giant ficus tree methodically dropped filth on the cars beneath it. I wanted to leave the whole thing, the sickness, the torments. To find a healthy life, to do something positive, to take care of somebody. Maybe in Australia, but not here, no, it couldn't happen here . . . This lasted no more than a few seconds until Haim called and asked for an update.

"I'm going up to him," I said.

Now I was alone with Hani in Daphna's apartment. I watched replays of basketball games. He was out of it and now and then he sank into sleep, woke up, asked a few things and dropped off again. I had once thought of going to one of those big games. But where would I go after the game? To a cheap hotel near the railroad station? The street lights would come into the room through the window, drunks would yell from downstairs on their way to the night train, I wouldn't be able to sleep.

I helped him go to the bathroom, we walked very slowly, he smelled of the end now. I supported him under his arms, and I felt all the bones in his ribcage.

"Where are they?" he asked in Arabic. "Where are Daphna and the boy?"

I told him about the stabbing in the ass, a little jokingly, but he didn't laugh. "Oh!" he said, hit his forehead, and went back to Arabic: "The poor boy." It tickled me to talk with him in Arabic, to go over to his field, so he wouldn't have to make an effort for me. "He was the most beautiful boy you ever saw," said Hani. "And smart. He could talk when he was a year old. The kind of boy you say will save the world when he grows up. That he'd do everything we couldn't. And look what he became. Ay, really that's enough already . . . " He shut his eyes, went back to the sofa, his face was full of bristles.

"He didn't say a word to me, the boy, ever since I came here," he went on muttering with his eyes shut, in his pleasant Palestinian dialect. How does he know I understand him? Maybe he intended to talk to himself. "All the time in his room or yelling at his mother to give him money, complaining to her, once we came together near the kitchen and he raised his hand to hit me. I carried that boy on my shoulders when he was a baby, I made him crushed tomatoes, as we do, and fed him very slowly with a spoon. I read him stories so he'd learn a little of our language, get used to the music of Arabic. Now he hates everybody. Even me. Hatred has taken over all our children and I'll leave here and won't be able to get it out of their heart."

When his breathing became heavy, and he started muttering visions in his sleep, I made a tour of the apartment. I went into her room, where her bed was covered with a colorful cloth. I sat on it a moment, lay down, felt the cotton weave of the sheet underneath. On the cabinet in the corner of the room were a few pictures: Yotam sliding in the park in the faded colors of a Polaroid print, cracked picture of a serious beautiful woman, apparently her mother, a couple hugging at a table on the seashore, maybe in the port of Jaffa, a sailboat in back, Daphna with long hair and big sunglasses, the very thin dark man. That's Hani, I told myself happily, he's that bastard in the picture, having a fine time with her.

Afterward, I sat in the breakfast nook, read the pages she had left on the table, her new stories, delicate and slow descriptions, things that happened a long time ago, or that would happen in the distant future. Nothing came together for a plot but a shadow of magic and mystery rested on every sentence. I was scared when I heard him suddenly call my name over and over, feverishly.

I went to him and stood at his head. "I want to see my son," he called out in a loud and clear voice, as if he were dictating a fateful decision. "I've got to see him before I die."

I held his hand, promised to help him.

"I'll talk to him now on the phone, bring me the phone," he said with a ravenous hunger, with gleaming eyes.

"Help you dial?" I asked.

"No, give me," he said, he sat up on one elbow, dialed a long string of numbers he knew by heart. The conversation revolved in space and descended to the depths of the oceans, long beeps of waiting, until a happy smile I hadn't seen before spread across Hani's face. "Hello, *ya ibni*," he said and then a charming conversation developed between a father and son that made me envy every word. He didn't pay attention to my presence, he was completely absorbed in talking. Through the receiver, I also heard the ring of the son's voice, firm and virile and warm. He asked Hani soft questions, what he did today, what he ate, and how he felt. He knew his father was in Tel Aviv, among the sons of apes destined to become mincemeat, but he didn't ask a word about us. He'll be a distinguished prey. "I want to meet with you," said Hani, I held my breath, the whole project now stood on the point of a word. The son laughed on the other end of the line. I went to the kitchen, as if to get something, not to rouse suspicion.

"No, I'm serious. Why don't we meet outside, so I can see you one more time," said Hani in the distance. Then he fell silent. The son talked a long time, things I didn't hear. "Just for a few hours," Hani pleaded. "You won't even have to stay overnight. We'll sit in a café, we'll talk. You don't know how much I want that. Afterward I'll be able to sleep in peace. Why not, my love?"

Now it will fail, I thought. The guy will understand immediately.

"Tomorrow," said Hani with a smile. "But not too late. My time is short."

I came back from the kitchen with a bunch of grapes. "So, what did he say?" I asked innocently, as if I didn't understand a word, and Hani answered: "It will be fine. You can buy tickets. I think he'll agree."

"Will your daughter come, too?" I asked.

"No, she can't leave her children," explained Hani, and sat down, steadier now, to take grapes from the bowl. "But you, *habibi*, you'll come with me. I want you to meet my son. I love you like a member of my family, as I love Daphna, and I want him to know a Jew like you. Maybe that will get a little hatred out of his heart. I can't go alone. I need someone to go with me."

Suddenly a feeling I didn't know came to me. An enormous wave lifted me, high and very strong, I was afraid to fall, I couldn't keep my balance, I gave into it, galloped on, and said with a broad smile I couldn't repress: "I'll gladly come with you, Hani. Tomorrow I'll buy tickets for us."

I made him a cup of tea, I picked a little mint from the plant in the kitchen window, poured a lot of sugar in it. He gulped it thirstily. "Ah, that's good," he sighed. I covered him well with a blanket because the frost had once again seemed to penetrate his bones.

"Tomorrow morning I'll buy tickets for us," I said again.

Hani held my hand and fell asleep. I saw a smile on his lips.

Daphna called as I was gazing at something on the screen. "How is he?" I asked.

"Like a person with an X carved on his ass," she sobbed again. "Maybe tomorrow they'll let him out. The wounds are superficial, there'll be a scar. But where will he go from here, it's so awful . . . "

I was holding Hani's emaciated hand but my fingers groped for her heavy rings, sought the softness in her. I didn't try to say a word of comfort, I knew there was no point. I felt her grief clamp my chest with pliers. Never had I felt another person's pain like that.

Preparations for the trip began. In the meeting room of the partners they built a detailed model of Limassol of plastic and cardboard, and a big group, mainly men, gathered around it like a playing field. Now they talked of operational details. Where would we come from, where would we stay, where would the meeting take place. They treated me with kid gloves, like a bridegroom, like a *shaheed* before going out to an operation. The whole thing was built on me, but there were details they didn't tell me to keep things compartmentalized. For instance, which one of the people around me will shoot the guy in the head. And with what weapon. And what direction will he come from.

Haim was supposed to sit in the forward command post in Limassol. It calmed me that I wouldn't be only in the hands of those fops. They wanted me to hold a plastic soldier and move with it from place to place on the simulation table, from the airport to the hotel, in a toy car. Afterward, they pushed the curtains aside and showed a computer simulation, they asked me over and over if I understood. "Do I look retarded?" I whispered to Haim. They suspected me as I suspected everybody I ever mobilized. Now I was the one being mobilized. If I'm good, I'll get a sugar cube in my mouth at the end of the route. Their assumption was that he'd come there without bodyguards. He's walking around alone in the world, keeping a low profile, clean-shaven, dressed solidly, looking like a clerk, like all the real professionals of death.

In the middle of the meeting, my cell phone vibrated in my pocket. Daphna. I quickly left the room, so she wouldn't hear the tumult in the background. She sounded steadier, as if she were back to herself.

"I heard that you and Hani are going to Cyprus," she said forcefully. "Tell me, is that true?"

"Of course it is," I said. For a minute all the contexts were confused.

"Is that still in the framework of the game?" she asked.

"What game?"

"The game you started," she said. "Or have you already left it?"

"I'm a little busy, can we talk later?" I answered urgently. Somebody had been sent out of the room to watch me as I stood in the corridor.

"Well I'm coming with you," she said jubilantly. "I feel like going to Cyprus. I need some rest. You'll have your little meeting and then we'll go to the mountains, I was there last time a thousand years ago. There's excellent air there. Buy a ticket for me too. I'll take care of Hani and guard him too. You promised nothing bad would happen to anybody, right?"

"What about Yotam?" I burrowed into a wall in the corridor.

"He's improving," said Daphna. "The sweet doctor said the cuts aren't deep, he can be released in two or three days. There'll barely be a mark, because it's easiest to erase scars on the behind." Somebody had told Daphna about an excellent drug treatment clinic that had opened in Givatayim, run by a psychiatrist who trained at the Betty Ford Center in California.

It wasn't part of the plan for Daphna to come with us. I hadn't yet thought what would be after the action, how I could see her again. And now she's stuck right in the middle of the thing. "Tell me, Yotam doesn't need you now? You think it's a good idea for you to travel?" I asked.

"I'm going because of Yotam," she answered and suddenly there was total silence behind her and around me, too. "After this trip we can start taking care of him."

I went back to the briefing. I disturbed their game. I said we'd have a traveling companion on the trip. Naturally I couldn't hide that. They weren't happy, to put it mildly. That put in another and unknown element, another plastic doll, not an obedient one, not on a string. They wanted me to get her out of it. I answered that it couldn't be done, she was a stubborn woman, if I refused that was liable to screw up the whole trip. There were whispers on the side, they glanced at me obliquely, somebody was sent to persuade me, I told them again it was out of my hands. If somebody else wanted to try, they could be my guest. I gave them all of our names, ID numbers, I asked them to instruct the security people at the airport not to make Hani go through the normal humiliating route of the Arabs, if they want him to get to the plane alive.

"This afternoon, you'll have the tickets," an energetic girl with narrow glasses promised me.

"How do you feel?" Haim asked me afterward. "It's a one-way trip, you know. They'll shoot him right before your eyes. It won't be pleasant."

"That's my profession, Haim," I said. "You don't have to remind me of that."

"He deserves to die," said Haim. "Don't kid yourself. He murders children."

"I know, Haim, I have no doubt about that. You don't have to persuade me. I'm the one who kills them with my own hands, remember."

"If everything works," said Haim as we merged onto the freeway, "everything that happened will be forgotten. There will soon be a round of promotions and you're on the list. I got a commitment from upstairs. This operation is very important to everyone."

"I can choke somebody every day for them. No point wasting all the money on trips," I said and Haim choked on a nervous laugh.

"It's not the same thing." He coughed. "With them, it comes with satellites and disguises and European scenery. You can liquidate a hundred terrorists in the Kasbah, nobody will notice that. But see what enormous headlines their liquidation will make. People pay money to see a matador finish off a dangerous bull, books are written about it, they decorate him with flowers, but nobody wants to buy tickets for a simple slaughterhouse."

What could one do with a comparison like that. Haim got out of the car and I turned up the radio. Freddie Mercury sang "Love of my Life" as a show tune. The thought of the trip excited me. I breathed easier, as if we were already in the good air of the mountains of Cyprus. I went to the hospital to meet Hani's doctor. I knew Daphna would come to him before the trip, and I didn't want him to dissuade her from it. I stopped on Ibn Gabirol Street to eat a shwarma; I had some free time now, all I had to do was get on a plane and be natural. The rest would be done by others.

I waited outside the office of the department head. Through the door, I heard weeping, then a patient came out wailing into a handkerchief, a stunned and pale man was barely supporting her.

"Oh, it's you, the security forces have arrived." The doctor took off his lab coat. "If you want to talk, walk with me," he requested. "I'm late for a lecture at the university. Tragedies all the time. Once we wouldn't have told them until the end, now it's all a matter of lawyers and insurance, no place for sympathy."

I told him about the trip.

"He may not hold out," said the doctor. "He's really at the very end. There's not one healthy cell in his body. Is there someone who can pay to fly the body from Cyprus?"

We entered the colorful shopping center next to the hospital, which was decorated for the holidays, you didn't know where you were with that whole colorful carnival of merchandise and disease.

"You'll take care of him, right?" asked the doctor standing at the top of the escalator. "He's my patient. Don't come complaining to me afterwards. Who are you going to kill there?"

My hands tensed to shut his mouth. Where else are people allowed to talk freely like that? Not even in America is such license allowed. I came very close to him. His eyes were frozen, mocking. There were a lot of people around us and the law also protected him. "Nobody will be hurt, all right, doctor? In the final analysis, we're trying to make sure that floor of the shopping mall stays clean, without pieces of flesh, that it will be possible to shop in peace, buy new year's gifts, children's songs, you know . . . "

He put a hand on my shoulder, as if he were about to give me the tidings of Job, too, and said mildly: "Don't get excited, I won't talk. I know where I live. And you've got to calm down a little before the trip. Your nerves are shot. Go rest a little, my friend," and he was swallowed up in the dark entrance of the parking lot.

I really did feel washed out. I sat at the polished counter of a high-priced café, across from me was a big mirror I tried not to look into. Somebody behind me was riding on a scooter for old people, with messy gray hair and hospital pajamas. There was something familiar about him. I looked again, it was Shmulik Kraus, after "Golden Doll," after the blows, after everything. Nobody was with him, I didn't understand how he got here by himself. I almost said to him: Regards from Hani, you remember, the guy from Gaza, he met you several years ago in "Watermelon Café," on the seashore, where you used to sit with the whole group. "That's Shmulik Kraus," I whispered to the young salesgirl, "ask him what he wants." I got a vague look from her.

I finished my espresso in one gulp which seared my belly. Since I was already there, I decided to go back to the hospital to visit Yotam. I went into the bookstore and bought him a new translation of Hemingway's *The Sun Also Rises*, and some chocolate; suddenly I felt sorry for him.

Yotam was lying on his back, alone, in a blinding light streaming in from the window. When he saw me, the automatic, mocking smile appeared, looking like an open wound. That's how he must have smiled at those who cut him, and they didn't understand. I sat in the armchair next to the bed, gazing north toward the Reading power station; that city really cried for help from the deluge that had descended on it. A beautiful Russian nurse came in to record something on his chart, she looked at me suspiciously, asked if I was his brother or his father. Yotam asked her wearily to put more drugs into his IV, it was murderously painful, and she said she'd ask the doctor because he had already gotten a lot.

The patient in the next bed was holding a transistor radio broadcasting news in a language I didn't understand. His pajamas weren't fastened properly and revealed all kinds of parts of his body.

I gave Yotam the book, even offered to read a little of it to him, if he wanted. "Hemingway," he chewed the syllables slowly. "How does she look, that bitch, can you imagine that drunken woman?"

"I think she had brown hair," I said. "And long legs. But a little full. And a great face. Maybe she was a blonde, I don't know."

"I think she looked cruel," said Yotam.

I wanted to tell him he should go into rehab, that it was a shame to waste his life, but nothing came out of my mouth. I offered chocolate. He turned his head away from me, left his long thin back to me, his spine protruding, his shoulders withdrawn, a thin bulb of hair. I picked up the book and started reading, there were a lot of things in it that I didn't remember. The young doctor came into the room, asked him to turn around, gently checked the dressing. "As far as I'm concerned, you can go home tomorrow morning," she said. "The wounds have healed nicely. In the end, it wasn't very deep. Only a slight scar will remain."

I offered to bring him soup or something, but he wasn't hungry. I recalled that I hadn't yet talked about Nukhi Azariya, hadn't asked him for an account of the attack; you can't leave something like that open. Mainly I wanted to prevent the negative molecules that carry inactivity to get into my brain in the form of bad thoughts. I got up to go and then he turned in my direction and opened enormous, frightened eyes, and looked without blinking, very deep inside. I put my hand on him to calm him, to feel that there was still a soul in that creature.

I went from there to the final briefing. Afterward I went home to pack a small travel bag.

We got to the airport in a taxi. I could feel that we had a tail all the way, there were all kinds of sensors stuck on me that turned me into a human antenna.

I pushed Hani in a wheelchair in the marble halls. Daphna wanted coffee. I suggested we drink after we went through passport control. We advanced as a trio to the security check. Hani became a little nervous and asked what was going to happen here. I calmed him. Indeed, everyone had been properly briefed. The girl sent to us was polite and asked only a few questions, why he was traveling (Hani answered the truth: "a family meeting"), and she asked us only if we had packed our bags ourselves, as if it's an everyday custom for two Jews to accompany a sick, old Arab to a family meeting in Cyprus.

Summer vacation was over and the holiday season hadn't yet begun, so the plane was small and half empty. Daphna sat between me and Hani and was in an excellent mood, as if we were going on a two-month vacation to the Caribbean and not for a day and a half in Limassol. Hani was excited, his hands shook and he was sweating, his face was awfully ema-ciated and you were afraid it would rip apart at every grimace of a smile. I was glad I was showing them a good time. Daphna had dressed him well, in a gentleman's clothes, and combed his hair carefully. Somewhere, a few rows behind us, sat the people who were tailing us. I had to be careful of everything I said.

Hani fell asleep, he was full of tranquilizers. The plane taxied down the runway and when it took off, I felt Daphna put her long, aristocratic hand in mine. I didn't care if the people behind saw us. I felt that she was inside me now, and I was filled with warmth. That's how we sat for thirty-five minutes until we landed in Limassol.

I rented us a big, high car, almost a jeep, and the two of them sat in the back seat. Now and then I looked at her in the rearview mirror. She was beaming, there was no hesitation in her, and every one of her looks tore me up inside. Hani was belted in and didn't budge, his almost dead body would be held together by a thread of soul until the final meeting. Now she held Hani's hand, and I was the driver in their last pleasure trip. The great summer heat had already passed here, there were wispy clouds in the sky hiding the sun now and then. We drove on the coast road between rows of palms with the sea sparkling behind them. Everything in Cyprus was clean and more airy, almost as beautiful as in Lebanon.

Our hotel was at the end of the boardwalk, at the edge of the city, in a grove of conifers. They chose it well, for it suited the purpose of our stay. There were four stars on its wall, but neglect could be seen immediately, as if there hadn't been any improvements and the furniture hadn't been replaced since the seventies. Daphna liked that. She laughed when we entered. The clerk at the reception desk looked at us, trying to understand, who is the man here and who is the woman and what is the role of the emaciated man in the wheelchair, of the dying man. And maybe he knew everything from the start.

We got two adjoining rooms on the third floor, with a view of the sea, one for her and Hani and the other one for me. Daphna opened the door to the balcony, pushed aside the curtain, and a great breeze came in. I rolled Hani onto the balcony. He shut his eyes and smiled. The blue bay was spread out before us, distant freighters honked in parting. We leaned on the banister and Daphna put her arm around my shoulders, as if she were my man. Beneath us was the hotel swimming pool, almost empty, because the big groups from the cold countries had already left. Around the hotel was a garden full of Mediterranean plants, and beyond it the modest houses of Limassol.

"We'll go there tomorrow," said Daphna and pointed to the high mountains crowning the bay. "There are wonderful groves there." I almost asked her: What are you talking about. There is no pastoral end to this tour, the whole thing is a delusion . . .

Daphna gave Hani some water, patiently and gently, stroked his head, brought a blanket from inside to wrap him in and sat close to him. His eyes were open to the sun, his nose sniffed the air, his hand didn't move from hers. I drank a beer from the mini bar and looked at the sea and the trees and Daphna, who looked like a French movie star in a Nouvelle Vague film. Hani said it was a good idea to meet his son here, in the hotel, very beautiful here and quiet.

"Where is he coming from?" asked Daphna.

"Syria, Syria. Tomorrow morning he'll come."

"I've never seen him," said Daphna and looked at the bay. The blue shirt she wore waved around her body in the sun. "Yotam doesn't know him either."

"Maybe after tomorrow . . . ," muttered Hani.

I was silent and drank my beer. Daphna brought him the medicines and his head fell back in sleep. I have to keep him alive at least one more day, and then they'll forgive me everything, I can go back to the cellars and the routine.

"He's awfully grateful to you," said Daphna. "He's a noble soul. So are you."

I looked at her uncomprehending. She does know who I am. She has to guess why we're here.

Time passed slowly. My eyes also closed, the sun charred the skin slowly and pleasantly. In the afternoon, the sea grew rough, and in the small jetty next to the hotel, the boats bobbled on the water. Daphna said she wanted to go down to the pool. "Fine, go," I said. "I'll stay with Hani."

I looked down at her when she took off the white hotel robe and put it on the chaise longue, bent over to check the warmth of the water, raised her head to look for me and waved. Then she stood on the edge of the pool, straightened up on tiptoe, the full purple bathing suit she wore stretched, she dove into the water as supple as a spring and left a long wake of smooth movements behind her. Hani was sleeping in the room, murmuring in his sleep all the time, God knows what he was dreaming about. One of the instruments connected to me beeped; a woman's pleasant voice said the package would arrive tomorrow at nine in the morning, final.

I looked far off into the sea, rows and rows of manes of foam, and I looked for Israel. I thought, what will happen afterward, when the ambulances arrive at the hotel parking lot, when Hani asks why his son is late and what's all that noise all of a sudden. Maybe he won't ask for an explanation because the whole drama will take place before his eyes. Whatever happens, that will be Daphna's problem. She'll have to explain to him, take care of him when he collapses. I won't be here anymore.

I followed the trail of the wind from the movement of the treetops. Cars turned on their headlights on the coast road. The air was perfumed with jasmine and a burnt smell. Downstairs, Daphna came out of the water, shook herself, wrapped herself in the robe, sat down on one of the chaises longues and stretched out her legs, fastening the belt of the terrycloth robe. I searched for tails on the balconies. On the second floor, a girl was sitting on the balcony with a newspaper and looking toward the pool. Now and then, she looked up, seemingly indifferent, and muttered something. I made sure Hani was sleeping and went out to the deserted corridor; I had to escape from the room for a little while. The elevator declared its arrival with a jarring beep, and when the door opened, there was the yachtsman, really sunburned, as if he had come here on a yacht. I was scared as if I was caught red-handed. "Good evening," he smiled at me calmly, and I answered, "Good evening," and almost turned around to go back to the room. Everything's exposed to them, I said to myself, she's swimming before them like a fish in an aquarium. How can they . . .

"Have a nice evening," the yachtsman parted from me when we got to the ground floor, and disappeared immediately.

I nodded to the clerk at the reception desk, sat down across from him in a deep armchair and pretended to read *The Nicosia Telegraph*. When the area was secured, I went out to the square across from the hotel, which was lighted with some high street lamps but looked dark. The salty smell of the sea blended with the sweetness of the plants in the garden, and the waves sounded close. Here they'd meet him, apparently with a gun to his temple, at very close range, he'd be folded up quietly on the square covered with twigs, as soon as he got out of the cab. When that happens, I'll be in the getaway car that will take me from there to the boat waiting in the harbor. I returned to the hotel and went down to the deserted pool, even the tail had disappeared from the balcony. I sat on a chaise longue and shut my eyes. I opened them when the sky was black and full of stars.

"Where were you?" laughed Daphna when she opened their door to me, wearing a beautiful black dress, her hair gathered up. Hani waved to me from the armchair in back and he also looked ready to have some fun. I took a step back. This was not in the plans. "Come, come in," Daphna invited me, and her gold earrings sparkled in my eyes. "We were waiting for you," she said with a smile. "Let's go out to eat. We're starving to death."

It turned out that Daphna had already checked with the clerk at the reception desk, who recommended a restaurant on the boardwalk, within walking distance; they serve good fish there and play Greek music. She put a thin sweater on Hani and helped him sit in the wheelchair. "Go change clothes," she urged me. "And don't look so depressed. We're here on vacation."

I hurried to my room and changed from gray trousers to brown trousers, and from a blue buttoned shirt to a light blue buttoned shirt. Those were the clothes I had planned to wear tomorrow, for the final act. I looked at myself in the mirror. I would have to take the tension and worry off my face immediately if I didn't want to spoil the whole thing.

We walked from the end of the boardwalk toward the center of town. The bay was open before us and the wind was clean. Daphna was gorgeous, statuesque; people looked at her as at a queen. I pushed Hani in the chair and Daphna walked close to us. "Go slowly," she said quietly. "Let's enjoy the walk."

The restaurant was almost empty. The owner was sitting at the entrance behind a wooden desk, and looked bothered by something. In the pictures surrounding him, photographs of local celebrities, you could see the trail of his old age. Daphna requested a table on the balcony, overlooking the sea. I peeped through the door to see when my companions would come in; they didn't plan in advance for this evening outing; they assumed that Hani would be too tired and weak to leave the hotel. The waiter came to offer drinks. I ordered a bottle of local white wine and some hors d'oeuvres. Below us dark, calm water came and went. Hani muttered something, I went close to him, he said in Arabic that it looked like Haifa here. I asked when he was in Haifa. "Ask her," he said with a smile. I didn't bring him back to Hebrew, it was more comfortable that way.

"When were you in Haifa?" I asked Daphna in Hebrew.

"In Haifa?" she laughed. "Oh, that was a long time ago." Her face was beaming. "We went on a big tour of the Galilee, Hani wanted to see Israel. We traveled for a week. A friend lent us his Subaru, one of those old, small ones. We took it up to Mount Hermon. Remember how I vomited on the way up, Hani? We went into places nobody heard of, we saw antiquities, we walked in rivers, in water, it was spring then and the snow had melted, the fields were full of anemones . . . "

"She was the most beautiful woman in the world," said Hani in Arabic. "Not even in my dreams did I meet a woman like that." Somebody should have collected his words in a box of treasures and wrapped them in cotton, because they were the final words of a poet.

"And on the last evening, we ate in Haifa, in a restaurant in Bat Galim, which must have gone out of business a long time ago," said Daphna, and put her hand on his, two such different hands, both long and delicate. "We ate fish, then we went to sleep in some crappy sailors' hotel in the lower city."

"We should have stayed together," said Hani in Arabic, quietly.

I poured the properly chilled wine. On the label was a vine on a rocky slope. The sea rolled to the stone wall beneath us and withdrew. I drank quickly because I had to lose myself.

"I want to touch him," Hani said suddenly. "Afterward, I can go. Don't give me too many drugs, so I'll manage to get up early. He's coming only for a few hours, that's what he told me. You'll see him, that man. You'll like him, you remind me of one another. The two of you are quiet and loyal. Come, give me your hand. You'll get to Paradise because of what you're doing for me."

I gave him my hand and he held it tight.

Daphna looked into my eyes until I trembled inside.

Some men sat down at the edge of the restaurant. You could see from a mile away that they were our tail. I laughed to myself as I drank, and Daphna asked what happened. "Nothing," I said. "I remembered a stupid joke I was told."

The food was good, the fried fish were fresh. I ate a lot; Hani tasted a little cheese and eggplant, and smiled sadly. I wanted to get up and run away from this cheap show, to go back where I belonged, where everybody knows exactly where he belongs. Calm down, you're starting to sweat.

Three musicians got up onto the small stage at the front, after they had been given supper. They slowly put out their cigarettes, took out their instruments. The group wasn't young, and they were dressed like clerks. They sat down, one with a bouzouki and one with a violin and the one in the middle held a drum and sang. As soon as he opened his mouth and plucked the first hoarse string, tears almost came into my eyes. That man, who looked like a customs official in the port, was singing only for me, about all my pains, as deep as possible.

"You aren't going to kill anybody tomorrow morning, right?" Daphna whispered in my ear in a soft voice that blended with the Greek, as if it was a verse in the song.

I let the song be played. We drank together, we moved to drink from the same glass, we had another bottle of white wine, we ate mullet with our hands from the same plate. Hani fell asleep and woke up and smiled at us, muttered something in Arabic. It was getting a little crowded there, a lot of locals came to hear the music.

We got up from the table at about eleven o'clock at night, when the evening was just beginning to get hot, but we had to put Hani to bed, fill him up with drugs again. I barely managed to wheel him in a straight line, the ground was spinning around me. I tried to hear the footsteps tailing us, I checked the cars driving by us, until Daphna hugged me, and together we pushed the wheelchair to the hotel, and nothing around us mattered.

We put Hani to bed. I took off his shoes and undressed him and laid his head on the pillows. I sat with him until he calmed down and fell asleep. Daphna leaned on the banister of the balcony. "Come here," she said quietly.

We watched the strange lights and the dark water, we came so close there was no distance, we kissed. We slept together in my room, on the broad white bed, with the window open, above the quiet rustle of the sea. The night was sweet as honey and broad as a golden pond, I sailed far away to a new world, a new world.

In the cold light before dawn, I was awakened by a muttered wake-up call in Greek. I remembered that something wonderful had happened to me, but the instructions of the operation immediately took control of me. The big battle started ticking, all around were all the assistants of the matador and the spies, and the listeners and the tails, and the sniper was also already taking care of his instruments not far from here.

I got up to shave and brush my teeth. The man in the mirror smiled at me like a bastard, with clear eyes; I loved that smile of his, before it was wrapped in the everyday gloom. Soon it will be six. I had to wake up Hani, prepare him for the day, the meeting, to sit with him at breakfast, cheer him up, tell him words of peace.

Daphna wasn't with me; in the middle of the night, she had parted from me to go sleep with Hani. "Tomorrow we'll go to the mountains," she promised.

Isolated cars were driving on the road, diligent Cypriots who got up early to go to work in the morning. Our guest was now in the terminal in Damascus, probably drinking a morning coffee. I got dressed and knocked on the next door. Daphna opened it, dressed in the hotel robe, a white towel wrapped her head like a makeshift turban. She smelled good, of toothpaste and soap. She kissed me. Hani was at the stage of putting on his pants. We greeted one another in Arabic: a morning of beans, a morning of cream. He couldn't stand up on his own, and his eyes were almost hanging out of their sockets he was so thin. He had the clear look of the world-to-come in his eyes. In another hour and a half, he'd sit in the lobby in the wheelchair and wait for his son who would enter with the confident stride of a man. I'll disappear a few minutes before, I'll say I have to go to the bathroom, to take a crap. That was the plan.

At seven, we were the first ones in the dining room. We sat at the window facing the bay. There was a lot of activity in the port, big ships were coming and going, honking their horns. Daphna brought an omelet and cheese and vegetables from the buffet. A waitress in a black apron offered us tea or coffee. I heard a humming sound all around, or maybe I only imagined it. The arena was sterilized. We sat alone in the dining room. Now there was no uncontrolled movement.

Hani told her she was as beautiful as a rose, as she put a piece of cheese in his mouth. He could barely swallow a crumb, and he coughed. "Awful empty here," said Daphna suddenly and looked around. "As if we were the only guests in the hotel. That's strange."

At that moment, a tall, older couple came in, two wanderers in shorts and walking shoes, and saved me the need for explanations.

"Maybe they serve lunch here," Hani said in Arabic. "Find out for me, please, reserve a table for four and we can eat with my son. We won't have to go too far. It's very nice here at the window."

"Wouldn't you prefer to eat alone with him?" I asked matter-of-factly.

"No, you're friends, I want him to meet you," said Hani with foggy eyes. "I want to put a little love in his heart."

We wheeled Hani's chair to the lobby. Daphna suggested we wait in the hotel garden, there were flower beds there and a little fountain and benches overlooking the sea. "Just bring Hani's hat from the room, and if it's not too much trouble, also a bottle of water and the bag of medicines I forgot," Daphna asked me with her sweetest look.

"Just don't go too far," I asked them. "I'll meet you in the garden in two minutes."

I went to the elevator. On the way I thought of my child and of Daphna and of the night that was, and the sea sparkled in my eyes. I entered the elevator, my jaw was clamped, and I pushed the button for the third floor. I knew I was being watched from every angle. I walked quickly, I opened the door of their room. Her clothes were scattered along with the instruments of his care, a smell of perfume mixed with a smell of disease. I looked for his hat and the bag of medicines, and a bottle of mineral water left over from yesterday, and I ran out.

In the garden there were narrow paths covered with pine needles, a little slide whose paint was peeling, and green ferns around high tree trunks, and flower beds growing wild, and benches facing the enormous sea. They weren't there. All the instruments of communication connected to the orifices of my body started beeping and yelling all at once. I ran back to the hotel and asked the reception clerk, panting, where the beautiful woman and the man in the wheelchair were.

They went out to the garden. He looked at me severely, that Greek. I thought about the little apartment he lived in and his wife and their children and how much money he got to collaborate. Or he was a Greek refugee from Famagusta and had no affection for Muslims.

I ran back to the garden, in a panic, and looked for them on other paths. I heard my name rising in the distance. They were sitting hidden behind a tangled and fragrant bush, under a thick tree, in a salty breeze of sea wind.

"Did you think we had escaped you?" she laughed.

I gave her the hat and the bottle of water and said they had to start going back to the hotel, he should be arriving soon. I knew if the son didn't see him waiting in the door, as they had agreed, he wouldn't get out of the car, and then the work would be more complicated. And they wanted everything to be clean.

"And who else is waiting for him up there?" asked Daphna, erect and serious.

I couldn't lie anymore.

"Me," I said.

"And you'll take care of him?" she asked.

Hani looked at me uncomprehendingly, and then his gaze filled with terror.

"You . . . "

I ran up the path with heavy legs, flew above the thin branches blocking the way, I had to be there, I couldn't run away. In the tiny earphone planted in my ear, I heard: "Two minutes to arrival." I slowed before the exit from the garden, entered the hotel calmly and sat down on the sofa. The parking area was spread out before me. I measured the seconds with my heartbeats. The reception clerk looked at me and went to pick up the phone. I saw silhouettes moving from every direction, in another minute they'd take shape and come out of their corners. And a white taxi is driving into the parking lot. Run, I was pushed through the glass doors, run, I dashed to the center of the drive, I jumped in front of the cab and waved my hands for it to stop. The driver got out and cursed in Greek and I burst into the back seat and closed the door behind me. The pavement in front of us suddenly filled with people bursting out of the walls and trees.

"Go, go back!" I yelled at him in English. "Fast!" I heard them connecting: currents passed through all the instruments, consultations in fragmentary words, how to stop them. "Go!" I yelled at him, and now we were on the coast road, on the way back to the airport, in the rush hour traffic of a regular morning.

I was breathing crazily. I looked to the right. He looked young and more vulnerable than in the picture, but his eyes were indescribably hard. I saw his eyes, and changed my mind. For eyes like that, I wanted to kill him with my own hands.

"Your father sends regards," I gasped.

He looked scared and groped for something in his pocket, forgot he had had to leave the gun before he got on the plane.

"The traitor, the shit," he said in Arabic and tried to find the door handle.

"No," I told him. "He didn't betray you. Your father saved you."

He looked around feverishly, suddenly everything seemed unstable. The two of us were in free fall without a parachute, without a hold. He opened the door quickly as the car was moving. I managed to shout at him, but he was already rolling on the side of the road, a curled up human ball. Honking started immediately, the driver looked in the rearview mirror and started yelling and cursing again, screeched to a stop on the shoulder. I sat inside another moment. I hoped he was dead, I wanted him to live for them. I got out and started marching fast along the guard rail, beyond it were the fleshy shore plants and a sparkle of the sea. On the road there was an enormous tumult, and the lights of the local police spinning. The driver shouted something and pointed to me. A moment before I was caught, a dark car passed by and a heavy hand came out and gathered me inside.

I didn't know when or how they took me back to Israel. I woke up in a small room on a kibbutz, or a boarding school:

bars on the windows, screens, a narrow bed, bare walls painted a greenish hue. Rustle of eucalyptus branches moving in the wind. I went to the door, which was locked. Outside sat a man in civilian clothes. I heard him whispering into a walkie-talkie, reporting that I had woken up. I felt refreshed, but not for long.

Two of them sat across from me at a simple wooden table of a kibbutz. They came in without knocking. "Get up, get dressed." I saw a solid look, a sturdy body, house in a village, SUVs and good-looking women—very normal people. They almost didn't use force, just were very cold, didn't ask how I felt, shot questions and I replied. Now and then, they went out for breaks, I heard them whispering, laughing maliciously—as far as they were concerned, I was garbage. They asked a lot about Daphna, about Hani, they questioned me about Yotam. I told everything as it was, I didn't hide practically anything. Afterward, they asked about Cyprus, wanted the whole picture, minute by minute by minute. I tried to sit upright, to answer clearly, not to look broken. I remembered which detainees stirred respect and which seemed like human trash to me. I kept back only one thing, the memory of the night with Daphna. Here I lied to them: No, I didn't sleep with her. They said insulting things about her, and I restrained myself so they wouldn't notice I cared, so they wouldn't put their dirty hands on her. Sometimes, they showed up at night after a whole day of silence, they turned on the light, pulled me out of bed, wouldn't let me brush my teeth, I sat across from them in my underwear—by now it was a bit cool at night, and they wouldn't let me go to the bathroom so frequently . . .

Between the visits there were long hours of nothing, attempts to sleep in sweat and bad dreams, to guess what time it was, to recall the face of the child. Outside, the guards who sat on plastic chairs dressed in civilian clothes were replaced. They had small guns in their belts—students putting themselves through school by guarding the traitor. They looked tranquil, I could surprise them, split the skull of one of them from behind. But what for? Where would I go from here, in that big prison? Once or twice an hour, a patrol car passed along the barbed wire fence. I could smell the sea, pick out the limestone outcroppings in the distance.

The guards didn't come into the hut, they just looked at me from outside through the barred window with the screen. I asked through the bars for permission to call my child. Two of them ignored me completely, the third got up off his chair—he had a cell phone in his hand and chatted and laughed on it all day with his friends—came to the window with firm steps and whispered to me to shut up and not talk to him anymore. I understood. I shut up.

I counted the days between one dawn and another: two weeks had passed. I waited for something to happen. I prepared chapter headings for my defense speeches, for the day they'd bring me up before the judge, but I couldn't compose an orderly argument. Only faces and eyes I saw, and groans and voices of distress, nothing that could be conveyed in words.

On the eve of Rosh Hashanah, they gave me a *kippa* and a prayer book with a special portion of fish whose plastic wrapping said "Carp North African Spicy Style." At long last I had something to read. I got a lot of sleep because the interrogations had diminished in recent days. All evening and night I read prayers over and over, I got to Sukkot; I tried to decipher signs in them, I saw faces of God—a gloomy and fearsome man. Outside the guard was wooing some girl on the phone; he sounded like a coarse fellow and I hoped she'd disappoint him. Afterward, he stopped guarding and emitted snores that drove me nuts. My fingers itched to break his neck.

After the holiday, they transferred me to a police installation near Ramle, to a real detention cell, without a window, without trees outside, with a thin mattress full of fleas. The interrogations there were more formal, they took orderly minutes. They didn't let me wash or shave. I lay curled up, like a hairy, ugly fetus, and I thought of death.

They released me suddenly, one morning. A pale man sat across from me in the interrogation room and made me sign all kinds of forms. I was forbidden to talk about anything connected with the service, the operations of the service, the things I had done. I was forbidden to leave Israel. Forbidden to talk with journalists. A policeman accompanied me to the door of the station. The sun blinded me when I went out. I had a long beard, and my clothes were filthy and stinking. I had no money. They had also forgotten to give me back my watch. It took a long time to find a taxi that would take me in my condition. The driver asked what had happened to me. I was silent.

For three days I slept in my apartment, which was locked and deserted, the home of a family that no longer exists. I left the shutters closed. I couldn't read. There was nothing or no one on the shelves that could talk to a person in my condition. I spoke a few words with the child on the phone; I wanted that conversation so much but I choked up and couldn't continue. "When will you come to me, Papa?" he asked and his voice sounded distant, as if he was in another solar system. Sigi asked where I had disappeared, in a flat and hostile tone. "I've got something serious going with somebody, just so you'll know, I don't want you to hear it from the child. He misses you. Don't disappear like that again. You don't have to punish the child because of me."

When I managed to get up, I looked in the piles of papers that had accumulated at the door for some reference to Cyprus ,on or around the day we had been there, but I didn't find anything. Once I called Haim; that was stupid because he hung up on me, and about half an hour later, police knocked on the door and asked if everything was all right. They walked around the apartment and rummaged through my things. I had to disappear, be forgotten, buried in the earth in some God-forsaken corner.

When the summer ended, on the last day of October, I left the house for the first time. The boring suburban street, the dull houses, people I don't know. With every step, eyes stuck in my back like arrows. I drove to the city. I hadn't shaved off the beard I grew in prison, and I was pale as death. I missed her street, the beautiful ficus trees that made the sidewalks dirty, the crooked children of the city, the gloom of the staircase. I sought her warmth. I went up the stairs slowly, like the first time I came.

The big window was open and purple spots of sunset blew inside with the wind. We sat in the kitchen. "The *etrog* man returned," she said and stroked my head. It grew dark outside, but we didn't turn on a light.

"What's with Hani?" I asked.

"Dead," said Daphna. "A few days after we returned. Died here, in the living room. In his sleep. Yotam called to tell me. I wasn't home."

"Did he say anything?" I asked.

"He said thank you for saving his son."

"I don't know if I managed even to do that," I said.

"You did," said Daphna. "They were here, asked questions. Put me in jail for two nights. Not a pleasure, especially knowing that you were being held as well. I understand he got out of it wounded, but alive. Not so awful, he probably deserved to do some time."

"He's a murderer," I said. "I saw that in his eyes. I should have killed him there, in the cab."

"All of us are murderers," said Daphna. She was very thin and her eyes were sad. I went to the windowsill, smelled the plants, listened to the voices in the yard and the street. She sat shriveled up, barefoot, covered with some cloth. She said it was getting cool, but the rain didn't come.

"Where is Yotam?" I asked.

"He's here," said Daphna quietly. "In his room. He comes

out only at night. Takes money from me. Comes back filthy and shaking in the morning." I looked at the door to the corridor where the monster sits at the dark end.

"You should throw him out," I said angrily.

"I can't," she said. "He's my son. He's Hani's son. He's all I've got left now."

He sat drooping on the corner of the bed with his hair covering his face and small bloodstains on the sheet beneath him. It was a child's room and he filled it with the smell of a sick old man. I entered with firm steps and combed through the room. I checked the drawers and the hiding places. I crammed all the stuff I found into a bag. He shook himself and tried to get up and go out, pushed me. I shoved him to the wall. Daphna changed the sheets and cleaned the room quickly with a broom and a rag. He went wild and cursed and spat. I was very strong, I restrained myself, I tightened my hold so he couldn't get away. Daphna put a bowl of fruit and bread and water on the small desk. We went out together and locked the door behind us.

We sat in the kitchen to wait.

ABOUT THE AUTHOR

Yishai Sarid studied law at the Hebrew
University of Jerusalem and received a gra-
duate degree in public administration from
Harvard University. He works as an attorney
and contributes articles to the Hebrew press.
Limassol is his second novel.

Carmine Abate
Between Two Seas
"A moving portrayal of generational continuity."
—*Kirkus*
224 pp • $14.95 • 978-1-933372-40-2

Salwa Al Neimi
The Proof of the Honey
"Al Neimi announces the end of a taboo in the Arab world:
that of *sex!*"
—*Reuters*
144 pp • $15.00 • 978-1-933372-68-6

Alberto Angela
A Day in the Life of Ancient Rome
"Fascinating and accessible."
—*Il Giornale*
392 pp • $16.00 • 978-1-933372-71-6

Muriel Barbery
The Elegance of the Hedgehog
"Gently satirical, exceptionally winning and inevitably bittersweet."
—Michael Dirda, *The Washington Post*
336 pp • $15.00 • 978-1-933372-60-0

Gourmet Rhapsody
"In the pages of this book, Barbery shows off her finest gift: lightness."
—*La Repubblica*
176 pp • $15.00 • 978-1-933372-95-2

Stefano Benni
Margherita Dolce Vita
"A modern fable...hilarious social commentary."—*People*
240 pp • $14.95 • 978-1-933372-20-4

Timeskipper
"Benni again unveils his Italian brand of magical realism."
—*Library Journal*
400 pp • $16.95 • 978-1-933372-44-0

Romano Bilenchi
The Chill
120 pp • $15.00 • 978-1-933372-90-7

Massimo Carlotto
The Goodbye Kiss
"A masterpiece of Italian noir."
—*Globe and Mail*
160 pp • $14.95 • 978-1-933372-05-1

Death's Dark Abyss
"A remarkable study of corruption and redemption."
—*Kirkus* (starred review)
160 pp • $14.95 • 978-1-933372-18-1

The Fugitive
"[Carlotto is] the reigning king of Mediterranean noir."
—*The Boston Phoenix*
176 pp • $14.95 • 978-1-933372-25-9

(with Marco Videtta)
Poisonville
"The business world as described by Carlotto and Videtta
in *Poisonville* is frightening as hell."
—*La Repubblica*
224 pp • $15.00 • 978-1-933372-91-4

Francisco Coloane
Tierra del Fuego
"Coloane is the Jack London of our times."—Alvaro Mutis
192 pp • $14.95 • 978-1-933372-63-1

Giancarlo De Cataldo
The Father and the Foreigner
"A slim but touching noir novel from one of Italy's best writers
in the genre."—*Quaderni Noir*
144 pp • $15.00 • 978-1-933372-72-3

Shashi Deshpande
The Dark Holds No Terrors
"[Deshpande is] an extremely talented storyteller."—*Hindustan Times*
272 pp • $15.00 • 978-1-933372-67-9

Helmut Dubiel
Deep In the Brain: Living with Parkinson's Disease
"A book that begs reflection."—*Die Zeit*
144 pp • $15.00 • 978-1-933372-70-9

Steve Erickson
Zeroville
"A funny, disturbing, daring and demanding novel—Erickson's best."
—*The New York Times Book Review*
352 pp • $14.95 • 978-1-933372-39-6

Elena Ferrante
The Days of Abandonment
"The raging, torrential voice of [this] author is something rare."
—*The New York Times*
192 pp • $14.95 • 978-1-933372-00-6

Troubling Love
"Ferrante's polished language belies the rawness of her imagery."
—*The New Yorker*
144 pp • $14.95 • 978-1-933372-16-7

The Lost Daughter
"So refined, almost translucent."—*The Boston Globe*
144 pp • $14.95 • 978-1-933372-42-6

Jane Gardam
Old Filth
"Old Filth belongs in the Dickensian pantheon of memorable characters."
—*The New York Times Book Review*
304 pp • $14.95 • 978-1-933372-13-6

The Queen of the Tambourine
"A truly superb and moving novel."—*The Boston Globe*
272 pp • $14.95 • 978-1-933372-36-5

The People on Privilege Hill
"Engrossing stories of hilarity and heartbreak."—*Seattle Times*
208 pp • $15.95 • 978-1-933372-56-3

The Man in the Wooden Hat
"Here is a writer who delivers the world we live in…with memorable and moving skill."—*The Boston Globe*
240 pp • $15.00 • 978-1-933372-89-1

Alicia Giménez-Bartlett
Dog Day
"Delicado and Garzón prove to be one of the more engaging sleuth teams to debut in a long time."—*The Washington Post*
320 pp • $14.95 • 978-1-933372-14-3

Prime Time Suspect
"A gripping police procedural."—*The Washington Post*
320 pp • $14.95 • 978-1-933372-31-0

Death Rites
"Petra is developing into a good cop, and her earnest efforts to assert her authority…are worth cheering."—*The New York Times*
304 pp • $16.95 • 978-1-933372-54-9

Katharina Hacker
The Have-Nots
"Hacker's prose soars."—*Publishers Weekly*
352 pp • $14.95 • 978-1-933372-41-9

Patrick Hamilton
Hangover Square
"Patrick Hamilton's novels are dark tunnels of misery, loneliness, deceit, and sexual obsession."—*New York Review of Books*
336 pp • $14.95 • 978-1-933372-06-

James Hamilton-Paterson
Cooking with Fernet Branca
"Irresistible!"—*The Washington Post*
288 pp • $14.95 • 978-1-933372-01-3

Amazing Disgrace
"It's loads of fun, light and dazzling as a peacock feather."
—*New York Magazine*
352 pp • $14.95 • 978-1-933372-19-8

Rancid Pansies
"Campy comic saga about hack writer and self-styled 'culinary genius' Gerald Samper."—*Seattle Times*
288 pp • $15.95 • 978-1-933372-62-4

Seven-Tenths: The Sea and Its Thresholds
"The kind of book that, were he alive now, Shelley might have written."
—*Charles Spawson*
416 pp • $16.00 • 978-1-933372-69-3

Alfred Hayes
The Girl on the Via Flaminia
"Immensely readable."—*The New York Times*
164 pp • $14.95 • 978-1-933372-24-2

www.europaeditions.com

Jean-Claude Izzo
Total Chaos
"Izzo's Marseilles is ravishing."—*Globe and Mail*
256 pp • $14.95 • 978-1-933372-04-4

Chourmo
"A bitter, sad and tender salute to a place equally impossible to love or leave."—*Kirkus* (starred review)
256 pp • $14.95 • 978-1-933372-17-4

Solea
"[Izzo is] a talented writer who draws from the deep, dark well of noir."
—*The Washington Post*
208 pp • $14.95 • 978-1-933372-30-3

The Lost Sailors
"Izzo digs deep into what makes men weep."—*Time Out New York*
272 pp • $14.95 • 978-1-933372-35-8

A Sun for the Dying
"Beautiful, like a black sun, tragic and desperate."—*Le Point*
224 pp • $15.00 • 978-1-933372-59-4

Gail Jones
Sorry
"Jones's gift for conjuring place and mood rarely falters."
—*Times Literary Supplement*
240 pp • $15.95 • 978-1-933372-55-6

Matthew F. Jones
Boot Tracks
"A gritty action tale."—*The Philadelphia Inquirer*
208 pp • $14.95 • 978-1-933372-11-2